The Old Turk's Load

The Old Turk's Load

<small>GREGORY GIBSON</small>

The Mysterious Press
New York

Published simultaneously in Canada
Printed in the United States of America

FIRST EDITION

ISBN-13: 978-0-8021-2113-4

The Mysterious Press
an imprint of Grove/Atlantic, Inc.
841 Broadway
New York, NY 10003

Distributed by Publishers Group West

www.groveatlantic.com

13 14 15 16   10 9 8 7 6 5 4 3 2 1

For Fred Buck

The Street Brothers

The Street Brothers weren't really brothers. They were from LA, and they always worked together, and their names happened to be Woody and Vince. It was their East Coast colleagues who, for reasons known only to gangsters with ninth grade educations, had given them the "Brothers" handle. In the summer of 1967 they spent a long afternoon on the New Jersey piers producing documentation, dealing with brokers, paying fees, and filling out customs forms in order to take possession of a custom-built Porsche, "straight from the factory," via Marseille.

Woody passed the time by thinking about cars he had owned in the thirty-five years he'd been alive. His father had worked for the phone company and, what with the war, it wasn't like his family got a new car every year. He had childhood memories of a black '39 Packard—the way the trunk humped up in back—combined, somehow, with ice-cream cones and gas rationing coupon books. Then the '52 Chevy Fleetline—used but cherry, with full trim and Powerglide—his first car. The '55 Mercury Monterey, back to a Chevy in '57, Mercs again in '61 and '65, then his current '67 Lincoln with the tinted glass. It took a while to sort through the succession of models, with their accessories and combinations of tans, canaries, burgundies, slates, and leather, chrome or wood-grain finishes— interior *and* exterior. Woody had a habit of thinking in lists.

Vince, on the other hand, was adept at not thinking at all. Sometimes after a long silence Woody would say, "Vince, what are you thinking?" and Vince would reply, "Nothing." Woody liked that.

What Vince did was whistle, a thin, curling, barely audible stream of air. He'd hear a song on the radio and it would stick in his head, so he'd blow the first few bars over and over, for days on end, until another song replaced it. Right now he was on the Stones' "Ruby Tuesday." He'd get as far as "Still I'm gonna miss you" and start over. Invariably, Woody would be relieved when Vince picked up a new song, then annoyed for a few minutes at the prospect of hearing its beginning notes over and over. Soon he wouldn't hear it at all. They were made for each other.

The Street Brothers were in the compliance industry. They'd come east from Los Angeles fifteen years earlier and spent their entire careers in the employ of Mr. Angelo DiNoto of New Jersey, enforcing discipline among the loan sharks, bookies, whores, crooked cops, and compromised government officials who comprised DiNoto's empire. There'd always been drugs, of course, but things had been changing throughout the sixties. Now Mr. D.'s operation was more . . . refined.

Under pressure from the American government, Italian officials were cracking down on Corsican and Sicilian entrepreneurs. In Turkey, facing similar pressures, growers slowed poppy production to a trickle. Through the malign inadvertence of the CIA, the centers of opium production shifted to Southeast Asia. Yet the Turkish trickle—stuff that used to be referred to as "Druggist's

Opium"—was prime shit, the raw product yielding up to 20 percent morphine, nearly twice what was expected from Golden Triangle exports.

Accordingly, each season, on a remote Anatolian plateau at the farthest reach of Mr. D.'s influence, an old farmer set out a field of high-octane poppies—a million rapture factories. At harvesttime he and his people would move through the field, collecting the latex the plants gave up, licking the metal tool's edge to lubricate it, working in patient bliss, sunrise to sunset, day after day. The sticky brown goo would be carried by mule back to Izmir, by ship to Marseille. There it was boiled, limed, filtered, seared by acid, pressure-cooked in nasty pickle-smelling chemicals, chloroformed, carbonated, and squeezed till the god-stuff was tricked out, whored up. The old Turk's crop would be smack by then. Horse. Junk. Ten kilos of blindingly pure heroin.

They'd installed the 1967 load in the body of a customized Porsche specially ordered by an American businessman, and shipped it as a private consignment via United Marine Transport to Newark, New Jersey, USA.

It was nearly six p.m. by the time Woody got the keys and backed his baby carefully out from among the dozens of vehicles parked on the dock. Then he spent an eternity going over every inch of the car, inspecting it for scratches and nicks. In Vince's considered opinion, the guy had balls of steel.

When Woody finally gave the okay, they left the piers and drove slowly up Doremus, through the strange harsh odors of the industrial wasteland fronting Newark Bay. It was a long, straight road, and there was more than enough daylight for them to take careful note of anyone behind them. They stayed on Doremus over

Passaic to Market Street where they stopped for a leisurely dinner in a Mr. D.–owned joint with a window seat that gave them a view of their shiny new car. Then, when the evening was sufficiently advanced for downtown traffic to have abated, the Street Brothers headed west on Springfield Avenue, planning to take Route 124 straight up to the factory in Morristown where the goods would be cut and packaged. It was a milk run, but it merited every precaution because it had a significant potential downside. Their cargo, by the time it hit the retail trade, would yield $5 million.

Springfield Avenue runs uphill as it approaches the center of Newark from the east. The two men were cruising sedately up this hill when they encountered a crowd of people running full tilt down toward them.

There was only one car in front of theirs. Vince saw its tail-lights go on and said, "Now what?"

Then the crowd swallowed them. A trash can cracked the rear window. People began rocking the car. Woody drew his gun but the car rolled and in the chaos of being upset there was nothing to shoot at. Black arms hauled them onto the street. Angry eyes saw the suits and the gun, mistook the men for undercover cops. They were lucky to escape with concussions and bruises.

Earlier that evening, while the Street Brothers had been eating their dinners, the pigs had been making a rough and very visible bust on a cabdriver named John Smith. He was hauled into the Fourth Precinct station house where, as the rumor ran, further beatings led to his death.

In Newark, against a backdrop of poverty, unemployment, decayed housing, and discrimination, racial tensions had been ramping up all summer, and the locals were seething with frustration. The cops, while aware of this, were not sensitive to it. In fact, they didn't give a fuck what the niggers thought.

As it happened, the Fourth Precinct was just across the street from Hayes Homes, a large and particularly dysfunctional welfare housing development. When the residents at Hayes got wind of what was happening with their brother John Smith, they went into the streets. The cops responded by pouring out of the station like angry bees, maybe a dozen of them in riot gear, laying around them with batons, aiming to put people down.

However, to their considerable surprise, this time the people did not go down. After the first few heads got busted, bricks began to fly. More brothers and sisters came out and the infuriated crowd swelled—the papers said four hundred, but it was more like a thousand—pushing the pig back into his pen, then spilling down the scabrous blight that was Springfield Avenue, a single rage-drunk organism out to avenge three centuries of rotten history. That shiny bauble, the Porsche, with its two nattily attired honkies, was irresistible.

Smoot

Smoot made the papers twice that week.

The first time was on July 15, 1967—the third day of the Newark riots. There was a photo in the *New York Times,* widely reprinted, of looters carrying televisions and toasters through a broken department-store window. Its protective grate had been torn down and thrown on the sidewalk in a wavelike curl, adding an interesting design element to the left side of the photo. On the right side people stood and watched. Some wore looks of disapproval. They, presumably, were the good Negroes, the ones white America desperately hoped outnumbered their looting brethren. Smoot was in this crowd of onlookers, wearing his signature tight pants, white shirt, snap-brim hat, and shades. If you knew him, you'd right away recognize him in the photo. He was checking things out, hanging back and watching like he always did.

Three days earlier he'd been doing the same at the edge of the crowd laying the beating on Woody and Vince, and he'd stayed behind after the mob moved on, to inspect the bloodied victims rolling in a heap in the gutter. Those two guys weren't cops, he realized. Not in those clothes, not in that car. And though he didn't get a very good look at the gun before the swarm ate it, he could tell it wasn't no stubby .38 like the pigs used. He went to a pay phone in the Hayes and dropped a dime.

He got hold of his man, Julius Roth, who happened to be in town attending to accounts receivable on behalf of *his* boss, an independent New York real estate operator named Richard Mundi who had substantial holdings in the slums of Newark. Smoot told Roth there was something funny about this pair of white cats and their car. They looked mob, and the car was foreign, with foreign plates. So what was it doing in Newark, anyway? Roth thanked Smoot and told him to scram, to get lost and stay lost. Then he called Mossman. The two men put on monkey suits, borrowed a truck from one of their garages in the neighborhood, and hauled the Porsche away themselves, unnoticed and unchallenged in the desolation that followed the first wave of rioting, as if the bounty on whites had expired. They agreed with Smoot's assessment, and they took the car apart piece by piece until they found the ten plastic sacks of smack. The rolled-over car was dumped in a deep quarry in Pennsylvania and the old Turk's load put in a safe in Manhattan. Waiting.

Its rightful owners were pissed. They were out a quarter million dollars up front and twenty times that in the long run. Vince and Woody were beat up, but they could talk okay. Their story made it clear this had been nothing but a horrible accident. Still, someone had that fucking smack. The wise guys tore the town apart but couldn't find anyone who knew a thing. So they waited. Sooner or later, the shit would turn up or someone would squeal.

Roth was waiting, too, for something he hoped would never come to pass. He liked Smoot. The kid was different from the rest of those street spades. He sent Smoot $500, hoping he'd just fucking disappear. Without a word. Would realize what the deal was and pack his bag. Head to Oakland and join the Black Panthers. Do the Muslim thing. But far away. Put some distance between him and Newark.

It wasn't to be. For all his smarts, Smoot was missing a piece, like the missing "h" in his nickname. Roth figured he was just *that* short of Smooth.

The call came on July 17, the last day of the riots. Smoot asked how the deal with the fancy car went down. Very good, Roth told him. Smoot said he thought as much, seeing the way the Guineas was tearing up the town, musta been something they wanted bad in that car. Roth was silent. Musta wanted it bad, Smoot went on, 'cause they making it hot for everyone. Roth asked him why he didn't just get the fuck out of town if it was hot. Smoot, indignant, wanted to know how could he ax him that shit when he knew he'd be leaving his momma all alone in the Hayes like that? Roth asked him how much? Smoot, cool and confident, said five. Roth said next night at Riverbank Park.

But he had no stomach for it. He dutifully reported the conversation to Mundi and said he didn't want any of the action after that. Neither did Mossman. So Mundi sent Seamster, a soft-spoken, sandy-haired sadist with a taste for boys, who happily shot Smoot—though he wished he could have done more—and pushed the body into the Passaic.

The cops found the corpse after a couple of days, which was the occasion of Smoot's second newspaper appearance. Roth read the brief article in the *Star-Ledger*. He tried to tell himself that it was just the funny thing about the name that was hanging him up.

The kid actually was DiShaun Smoot. That was how they printed it in the paper. "DiShaun Smoot, age 23." And he really did have a mother. He'd lived with her in the Hayes. In truth Roth was sick at heart that the kid had turned greedy and then had to die. He was sick of the whole business. Burned out. Smoot was the beginning of the end for him.

John Smith the cabby, who had *not* been beaten to death by the cops, appeared on the cover of *Time* the next week, and was featured in the cover story, "Anatomy of a Riot."

Smoot didn't make it in that one.

The Situation with the Mailman

The way the Mailman figured it, taking that physical was the biggest mistake of his life. The grand scheme, as he'd originally conceived it, had been to start young at the post office, cash out early with a pension, then commence a free and easy life as a man of means. But after his twenty years of blood time were up, he'd had to submit to a physical exam to qualify for his discharge. It was his first visit to a doctor in decades, and the sudden intrusion of medical science ruined everything. They discovered that he had throat cancer and, after toasting him with radiation, they gave him a total laryngectomy with bilateral neck dissection. His oncologist, a man with a cancerous bedside manner, told him he had a 66 percent chance of making it to five years, and after that it was anyone's guess. The Mailman reckoned that if he hadn't taken the physical he'd have lived and then died. Like everyone. Now he was a Dummy, a Larry, a Neck-Breather—talking, when he was forced to, in his "bucco-esophogeal voice"—ghastly prolonged burps. No more Pall Malls, either. He'd always had a dark disposition, inclined to morose introspection, and the diagnosis confirmed everything.

He might have guessed what was in store for him; his father had died young of cancer, leaving him more or less on his own. In the excitement following VJ Day he'd drifted up to Gloucester, Massachusetts, and was sucked into a temporary position as a special delivery messenger for the post office. To his surprise, he liked the job and performed it well. It had a structure as foursquare as the city blocks he walked, and structure was important to him back then. The sadism, cruelty, and numbing bureaucracy of postal culture were bad, but no worse than what the world had already shown him. He moved up to substitute letter carrier, then floater, servicing the routes of five regular carriers on their days off, which allowed for a certain amount of planning. He started screwing Faye Thursday afternoons, then moved in with her—to the envy of the regular carrier, whose compulsive womanizing occasionally got him beaten up by irate husbands, boyfriends, and fathers.

In those early post-office years discipline had been looser. There was always time for small talk, and the Mailman visited other kitchens than Faye's. When it got hot, he'd leave a pair of cutoffs in the green relay box on Puritan Court, and stash the bag and his uniform in the back room of Cap'n Bill's underneath the Puritan Hotel. He'd sneak through the side lot of the Tarrantinos' on Beach Court, down Woody Curhan's cinder driveway, and slide into the cool green murk of Gloucester Harbor. He'd swim around Fort Point to the pump house in front of Cape Ann Fisheries, where Cominelli, the crippled oiler, would spot him and yell, "Hey, Mailman! Where's my fucking disability check?"

That was then. Now he couldn't even take a bath because there was no way to close the blowhole they'd cut in his throat. Two tablespoons would drown him.

After a few years the regular carrier retired and the Mailman got his route, which took up about twenty-five square blocks in the middle of Gloucester, extending from tony rich folks' houses on Middle Street to gritty squats on Columbia, two blocks over from Faye's place. At this point the Mailman conceived the grand scheme regarding his postal career.

Scheme or no, Faye eventually grew weary of his dark moods and took up with Schultzie, scion to Schultz Brothers, the local trash barons. Schultzie was a much nicer man. The Mailman moved across town, into the basement apartment of a four-family tenement on the back side of Portugee Hill. The basement suited him fine, though he'd occasionally stop in at Faye's for lunch or a visit, since the route was still his. Sometimes he'd even have a beer after work with Schultzie. It was amiable, subdued. They would've let him farther back in, but he kept his distance, like a waterfront cat. The route satisfied whatever need he had for attachments.

There were 630 souls on his route. He'd once saved Mrs. Alves who'd fallen in her living room, even though her family thought he should've let her die there. And he'd witnessed, helpless, the fatal heart attack of Cummings, the ward councilor. He knew where Sammy the Rat slept it off, and could follow Sammy's slime trail at eight a.m. down to the Dugout, where he'd take his first, trembling drink with the night shift fish packers from Gorton's just getting off work. The Mailman hadn't delivered a baby, but he'd witnessed Dickie Lufkin being born in the backseat of a car that never even got started for the hospital. And kept a watch out for the Old Gal who got her daily beating from her boyfriend till she finally moved out, only to have him start beating her at her new place. The cops found him dead one night in the parking lot, but they declared he'd slipped on the ice as he was getting into his car. The Mailman knew the truth, and the Old Gal knew he knew. The whole route was like a spiderweb, and when a gnat hit the sticky the spider knew, and when the spider moved the gnats knew. "Mailman! You fucked my girlfriend/saved my mother/saw my brother die/help me/get lost/ where's my check?" These connections were fulfilling in a certain way, but they were also intense—which, perhaps, was why people in his line of work had been known to go postal.

After he recovered from the surgery that marked the end of his career, he took a part-time job at the Gloucester Historical Association. The imposing clapboard Federal-style building had been on the far edge of his route, and once he'd realized what a perfect retirement tit it could be, he'd begun to integrate it into his grand scheme, taking care to suck up to the staff, doing extra favors, ignoring their condescending ways. Over time the Yankee bluebloods who ran the place came to rely on his trustworthy, unexceptional presence. They missed him when he dropped the route, sent him flowers in the hospital, and hired him when he got his health back. They started him as a maintenance man. Once he began spending extra time in their research library, there was no reason to object. He offered to index files of letters and newspaper clippings—tedious, eye-straining work too taxing for the dowagers and dilettantes who volunteered there. Punctual, productive, invisible. Within a year he had his own set of keys and the run of the place.

He'd discharge his janitorial duties in just a few hours, then work upstairs in the research library until the museum closed. He'd take dinner in his car, which required an hour's chewing and swallowing—far beyond the time he'd have been allotted at L'il Earl's or Ray-Joe's Pizza. Anyway, it freaked people out to see him eating in public. The food had to be cut into teeny bits and chewed exceedingly fine so it wouldn't strangle him. In the course of saving him from cancer, the docs had separated his esophagus from his windpipe. No more nose or mouth breathing. No nose blowing. If he got a cold he had to stuff a tissue up his snout. No more taste or smell.

When dinner was over he'd return to the darkened building to pursue what had become his abiding passion. He'd begun, just for the fun of it, researching the history of Faye's house on Church Street. When he discovered that it had been moved in the early 1800s from a few blocks away, he grew curious about the neighborhood. Using old maps, letters, newspapers, drawings, and documents, he reconstructed the history of the houses and families in that corner of his delivery route—back through the 1880s, when the fishing port had been in her prime, to the Civil War, the War of 1812, the Revolution, and beyond—down into that archaic era when every settler could be named, and thus each one loomed like a giant in history. He was certainly no historian—being only dimly aware that such a discipline even existed—but he had the instinct and, by some miracle, the passion. Building on his intimate physical knowledge of the city, the Mailman was re-creating it, street by street and family by family. Now when he walked the streets of his former route, he'd be just as likely to see it in 1767 or 1867 as in 1967.

He told himself it was just a hobby, a balm to his lonely days. But not too far beneath was the awareness that he'd somehow gotten himself trapped in a present in which there seemed to be no hope, no possibility beyond grinding, stupid repetition. The past afforded the Mailman his only feeling of release. The small pleasures of its continued discovery got him out of bed each day.

This depressing situation was enhanced by the unfortunate fact that, as a side effect of having his voice box cut out, the Mailman had acquired a nasty addiction to painkillers. With the help of his historical pursuits and his own fundamental toughness, he was managing it. But just barely. At the age of forty-two he was on his way to becoming a junkie.

Let It Be, Leave It Alone!

Although he'd spent most of his life in Manhattan, Walkaway Kelly emerged from his building as if he were landing on an alien planet. The rock beneath him and at his sides surged as he walked, in massive dizzying waves that disappeared when he stopped to watch them roll. Menace hung in the air, a sense of imbalance.

He put his head down and trudged east on Fifty-Third, aware that something had seriously disrupted the invisible currents guiding him through the world. Probably that mess he'd gotten into with the transvestite hooker and the German tourist. It hadn't felt right at the time, but events had swept him along and now he was on the other side, lying low, as if there were a chance of staying out of fate's way.

Eight days before, outside the Five Spot, a statuesque hooker and her john had brushed past. Tight dress, big hair, long legs, fuck-me heels—perfect except for her Adam's apple, but there was nothing to be done about that. When Kelly spotted the hooker at New Lefty's later that night with another guy, he was curious enough, in an amused sort of way, to sit a few seats down the bar from them and listen, checking them out every so often in the mirror behind the bottles. The new john had a heavy accent and was seriously drunk. He was a head shorter than the impressive she-creature and kept putting his face into her chest as he spoke, trying to nuzzle her. They disappeared after a while. Not long after, Kelly paid for his drink and departed, figuring that was that.

But it wasn't. As he passed the alley outside, he heard a noise that stopped him because it was not the noise that would've been made by a German tourist with an ampoule of amyl nitrate in his nose being blown by a good-looking transvestite who'd already slipped his wallet out of his pocket and was figuring how to peel off his Rolex while he came. It was a squeak of mortal terror.

Something different was going down. Instantaneously Kelly had the image of the other guy, the first john he'd seen with her, no john at all. The two of them were working the German over, going for the hotel key, passport, and traveler's checks. It seemed perverse to Kelly, using violence where sex would do. It called out for correction. He turned down the alley and found the hooker in front of a Dumpster with the now-limp German in a headlock, blood running from his nose. Her partner was going through his pockets.

The hooker saw him first. "Fuck off, asshole."

The other guy turned to face him. Kelly was in the groove now, and events were proceeding in slow motion, like the beginning of a car crash. He could see the punk trying to make him, trying to decide if he was a cop or not, and rendered that question moot by kicking him in the groin. The hooker dropped the German and came around in front of Kelly with a knife. She was headed for the end of the alley and slashed at him to clear her path. He stepped out of the blade's way, but the other guy rolled under his knees and Kelly fell back on the cobblestones, knocking his head so hard little stars came out. He knew he might go under. Then they'd do him.

That was when it dawned on him that he should have let it be, left it alone. The whole intervention had been a result of too much time on his hands; this was the kind of thing that happened when you forced matters. He pushed fast with his arms and legs, crabbing himself across the alley on his back. But they didn't come after him. The hooker and her buddy were long gone. He realized he was yelling, "Hey! Help! Hey!" like a human car alarm. People were gathering.

It took another hour to get the German sorted out. He was a businessman named Kramer, over here on some kind of real estate deal. Kelly gave him his card, and on the back he wrote whom to call at the cop shop, in the unlikely event the guy wanted to report the incident. Then he took a cab back to his place. His jacket was shredded, his shoulders were raw, his head was pounding, and his left ankle hurt.

He went to sleep for a couple of days, took hot baths for a couple more, then engaged in some light work at the gym. The ankle tended to get sore when he was on it for a while, but things were nominally okay. It just felt like he'd lost the beat, as if one unfortunate episode had knocked him off the wave.

Now he was headed for Sammy's Undersea Lounge, walking to get the ankle back in shape. The click of his heels on the pavement took on a reassuring rhythm and his surroundings reconstituted themselves as the known world. At Sixty-Second and Lex he ducked into comfortable darkness. Nets festooned the ceilings and the walls were hung with giant lobster claws, crab shells, sawfish bills, and stuffed octopus tentacles. A long aquarium behind the bar flooded the place with soothing blue light. Walking in there was like diving from the storm-tossed surface to the ocean's bottom.

He stood in the sawdust, waiting for his cherrystone clams, and watched the hands of Norbert, the burly man behind the bar. Forty years' immersion in cold water had turned them orange and pink, and prying shellfish apart had humped layer upon layer of muscular gristle over the joints. To Kelly the hands seemed like malign clams bent on destroying their brethren. With an instant's fatal pressure they'd slip the edge of the knife between the two halves of the shell, slit the muscles that held it together, scoop the quivering body loose, and flip the empty upper lid into the trash. After this operation had been repeated a dozen times, the hands set the platter of clams on the bar.

"Something the matter?" Norbert asked.

"Man's inhumanity to clam," replied Kelly.

And Her Name Was G . . .

She thought Gallagher was going to come but he pulled out and went down on her, so she faked a second orgasm, thighs slamming his ears. Then he got back inside her and worked the furrow in long rolling waves.

She was balling the well-known revolutionary Kevin Gallagher, but he was fucking Gloria Mundi, the millionaire's daughter, and he was giving it a lot more effort than she. Gloria let him toil away. She thought of broken glasses, coffee grounds, the beach and blue ocean, her far-away sisters in Southeast Asia or Latin America—on their backs for grunting imperialists and revolutionaries alike, all their lives somehow keeping that marvelous, quiet dignity. Wholeness. You could see it in their eyes. She thought of a lioness glimpsed in a scraggly zoo somewhere, not Central Park, but where else could it have been?

She'd been fourteen, just walking through, when she'd come across the lions doing it, the lioness a wiry, scrawny thing—just as Gloria had always thought of herself—behind black bars, getting down. The lion got his rocks in ten seconds and walked off to lick himself, but the she-lion kept rolling in the dust, ribs showing through like cage bars, no quid pro quo, no obligation to any king of beasts, or anything other than her own pleasure. Gloria recognized the absolute integrity of that creature. It made her insides tighten.

The swashbuckling Gallagher had come on to her as a savvy veteran of the culture wars. Like many rich kids, Gloria had been raised by predators and opportunists, and was an expert manipulatrix. She had little trouble getting him to escort her to the front lines of the battle, where she gained intimate access to the marches, demonstrations, confrontations, and endless fiery meetings aimed at bringing the established order down. She felt it was important to be doing something, to have *agency*. The world was changing and she wanted to be a part of that change. Besides, it felt glamorous.

That was also when she started getting tight with Irene Kornecki, an acquaintance from SDS meetings. Irene had been a law student when Gloria arrived at Columbia as an undergrad; now she was a lawyer, nominally a member of Kevin's inner circle, but more like an observer. She catered to conscientious objectors and movement people and was, in her careful way, as dedicated to change as any of them.

In the course of her dealings with Gallagher and his small band of activists (whom he called, in hip Latin American style, the *foco*), Irene began to engage Gloria's native intelligence. Soon she had her younger friend questioning the entire scene. Was it all about Vietnam? Okay, let's get out of there. But what happens then? Do we really want to "bring the war home"? Did Gloria really want murder in the streets? Had she ever killed anyone? Had she ever actually thought about it? Imagined the feel of hot blood on her hands? Had she ever wondered where Gallagher's rabble rousing would end? Ever stopped to consider that there might be different ways to introduce change into a hidebound system? And what *was* the system? Surely more than a bunch of white old farts—Johnson, McNamara, Hoover. What was its true nature? How had it ingrained itself so deeply?

As an inevitable consequence of this line of inquiry, Gloria began also to question her relationship with Kevin Gallagher. She'd naively assumed that she'd seduced him into granting her access to a secret and exciting world. But now she was beginning to realize that the only thing Kevin ever really did was run head trips on the people in the *foco* about who was the most committed revolutionary. It was all about power with him, which was all that the sex was, too. He was as big a bully as any of her father's thugs—worse, in fact. At least some of them supported families.

She'd already run her personal finances to the limit, posting bail for protesters and helping Irene research the cases of the most important political prisoners, and had felt fine doing it—a part of something larger than herself. But Kevin kept insisting on the need for funds, which forced her to have to keep explaining, in front of the others, that her own access to family capital was years away. It was humiliating. That was when she began to feel the first tug of a strange sense that grew stronger over the months.

There'd been many group discussions about money. Gallagher was all for stealing what they could from Mundi Enterprises. Gloria pointed out that the assets of her father's company consisted primarily of slums in Newark, New Jersey, which would be difficult to steal. So he switched tacks and went on a toot about kidnapping for ransom, an approved revolutionary tactic in Latin America and one much discussed of late in radical circles. He kept pressing her, digging for information about her father as well as certain company employees. When she told him that Julius Roth was the one man the company couldn't do without, Kevin got excited. They'd abduct Roth, he announced, and hold him at a remote spot. Maybe they'd kill him, maybe not. Gloria informed Gallagher that Julius Roth would be much more likely to kill *him*, and when Kevin actually got a look at the formidable Roth the idea quickly evaporated.

However, in the course of doing groundwork for a possible heist at Mundi Enterprises, Gloria found out about Daddy's windfall. This brought matters into focus.

Roth had spoken of the old Turk's load only generally, as an unanticipated situation over in Newark with huge potential and much risk. Her subsequent questioning of Seamster convinced her that Mundi Enterprises was holding something big. When he let it slip to her that the Mafia was posing a problem, Gloria figured it had to be drugs—what else would've belonged to the mob? Money or jewelry, maybe, but something that easy to convert would be gone already. Pot and acid weren't valuable enough. That left heroin or pills or coke. The bummer was that, full of pride at her own brilliance, she'd bragged about the Newark score to Kevin.

Now she was almost at the end of the long process of realizing how badly she'd been fooled by his square shoulders and intense eyes. He'd tricked her in some fundamental way. Used her, when all along she thought she was using him. Gloria was just beginning to understand how angry that made her. But it wasn't until she remembered the lioness that she understood the feeling that had been building inside her all these months. It wasn't anger. It was shame.

Kevin climbed off and went to lick himself. Gloria regarded him with intense distaste. Irene was getting inside her head.

The Situation with Kelly

Norbert was a keen student of human nature. He knew it wasn't enlightenment that made Kelly the way he was. Although he sometimes took on the amnesia of the habitual drunkard, Kelly's condition, in fact, predated his alcohol habit. His father, a journeyman welterweight called Irish Johnny Kelly, had prepared for his only child's birth by getting falling-down drunk. When the doctor handed over his newborn son, Johnny dropped him. Norbert knew the family, and that much was a matter of record. For the rest, he had developed a theory.

Norbert considered it likely that, after sliding headfirst through his father's slack grasp, the infant Kelly landed on the part of the brain that believes it knows what's going on and is always talking, talking, trying to get control of things—the part that most people listen to when they think they're thinking. This normally dominant chatter center could have been damaged by the fall, so the other, quieter part of the brain that is constantly in communication with the rest of the body—guiding it down the street, recording details it does not see, causing the hair on the back of its neck to rise for no apparent reason, flinching at a muzzle flash—that part could have assumed the functions of the conscious mind. This, in Norbert's estimation, might explain why Kelly spent so much time in the state of concentrated attention that precedes thought and so little in thought itself.

Certainly helpful in escaping the knives of enraged transvestite hookers (the story related in detail to Norbert over Bloody Marys), but of little use when dealing in any nonphysical way with those of his own kind. For Kelly, there were moments when the human universe was a distant galaxy.

What fascinated Norbert was how his friend had compensated. Shunned as a young man for his strangeness and ignored by both his parents, Kelly found solace and companionship in his father's pulp magazines and trashy novels. From Hammett he'd learned to present himself with unflinching directness. Chandler taught him how to crack wise while doing so. Cain presented sex as a sadomasochistic rite preferably enacted with distant relatives in abandoned churches. Spillane didn't teach him much of anything but gave him an ideal of womanhood, the beat-up dame. Further study of these masters provided Kelly with a store of scenarios—the jealous husband, the rebellious son, the too-greedy boss, the crooked official, the weak man brought down by his own vices—a thin array of archetypes for almost any human situation. A few empty years—echoing his playground isolation—on the police force in Bayonne had taught him how to maintain and operate a sidearm and keep his shoes shined. By then he'd grown into a light heavyweight version of Irish Johnny in his prime—cat-quick and possessed of a thunderous right. His education was complete.

The results, to Norbert's continual surprise, were viable. Kelly was a private detective by trade and had managed for more than a decade—by means of his unthinking courage, physical genius, and limited repertoire of canned responses—not to starve.

This raised an interesting possibility: Could it be that Kelly succeeded because most people's problems truly did conform to a few hoary stereotypes? If the husband was off the reservation, the official corrupted by his power, the wife murderously at the end of her rope, Kelly knew exactly what to say and do, chapter and verse. Was it possible that people, in all their twisted, self-absorbed dramas, were no more complicated than that?

Norbert respected Kelly—no, loved him—because he had cobbled a persona out of ill-fitting parts and, through his own indefatigable will, was making the ramshackle contraption work. If only, he mused, trundling more shellfish from the cooler, the man weren't so dense. If only he didn't act like such a jerk.

But even that had its good side. No one *ever* overestimated him. And, like the blade of Norbert's shucking knife, the leading edge of Kelly's physical intensity had no thickness. It slid again and again through the tightest interstices of tough situations, drawing the rest of him with it.

The Mailman's Best Friend

The Mailman had a croaker named Dr. Paulson who lived in a big Victorian house on Middle Street, a couple of blocks down from Faye and Schultzie's. His office was in the front room and if you had an appointment in the late afternoon you could smell his wife cooking garlicky dinner in the kitchen to the rear.

Dr. Paulson's chief concern as a physician was sodium intake. The Mailman would sit quietly in the comforting glow of the old shellacked wainscoting and Dr. Paulson would ask him how his throat was feeling. The Mailman would indicate that it hurt. Dr. Paulson would listen to his heart and tell him he was using too much salt. Then he'd write a scrip for two weeks' worth of morphine pills or Eukodol. The Mailman would come back five days later and ask for something else—Dilaudid, maybe—and Dr. Paulson would listen to his heart and advise against salt, writing the prescription without a thought. He made his living from customers like the Mailman, and by giving state-mandated physicals to bus and trash truck drivers in the employ of Schultz Brothers. The post office, under federal jurisdiction, had their own more competent doc a few towns away. He was the one who'd discovered the cancer. But after a while the

Mailman figured things out and got transferred to the care of his local physician, the senile stethoscopist, Oliver Paulson, MD. Since he filled the prescriptions by staggering them among a half-dozen area pharmacies, everything looked on the up-and-up.

Weekdays, the Mailman tried to keep to maintenance doses. But on Friday and Saturday nights he'd load up and go on his downtown ramble, working selected bars east along Main Street and returning westward via other waterfront establishments. This was as close as he ever got to recalling the pleasures of his old postal route—the recollection being always perfect, whereas the actual experience had often been marred by aggressive dogs, surly humans, the persistent pressure of the spiderweb. There weren't many mutts on the route of his ramble and, oddly, once he got the operation, they started liking him. Maybe it was the smell of meat.

The Mailman had a difficult time venturing on the streets sober. People gawked. At the bank or in the grocery store, it was a constant, hideous game of charades. When he was forced to speak, tellers cringed, children burst into tears. The doctors had tried to get him to use one of those gizmos you hold up against your throat, but there was so much scar tissue, he never found the sweet spot that made the gurgles resonate into speech.

Friday nights he'd quadruple up on whatever med was in supply, crush it in a soup spoon, mix it with Karo syrup, and swill it down with little gulplets of flat beer. Then he'd float from bar to bar, insulated, stoned, and silent, but *with* those around him in his drugged-up mystical way, drinking slow lubricating beers, empathizing, telepathing, reading entire life stories in new faces, the happenings of past weeks or months in the ones known to him.

Few conversations interrupted his reverie, but occasionally there'd be adventures. One Friday, just after sunset down at the Main Deck, a rackety bar built out over the water, a guy in full umpire regalia propositioned him on behalf of three not-bad-looking whores standing around the cigarette machine. The ump had just finished working a Little League game down at Boudreau Field but didn't bother to explain why he hadn't changed out of his dark pants and jacket and was still wearing his chest protector. Maybe he was expecting rough trade, or thought the outfit would be helpful in Friday night conflict resolution. Twenty bucks got the Mailman a blow job from June in the man's car 'round the side of the building. June was skinny, with a lean long face, and he came and came into it, in love at that ecstatic moment with her, his drugs, the bar, and the improbable ump.

Often there were more drugs—Sopors, to be taken carefully with beers, or rolls of downers imported, it was said, from Mexico, to be taken even more carefully—to lay him back into a deep velvety cushion of the evening, making everything a movie as flawless as his collection of recollections. More often it was dex and bennies—pills crushed and popped like Lik-m-aid. Coke was a high-end rarity in the bars he frequented, though once he got into some with a gracious fisherman friend at Kellehers. Couldn't snort it, of course, but did his gums sore with it. Then danced all night to Captain Jack Melquiez's squeeze box, winding up with a chubby, good-humored girl named Audrey who didn't mind doing all the talking and gave him a good fucking in her place over the Portuguese restaurant across from Pavilion Beach. She was a nurse at Addison Gilbert and he didn't scare her at all.

When the sun came up he left her asleep and walked off the last of the coke around the neighborhood called the Fort, then down to Fisherman's Wharf where he sat under the docks, bathed in the luminous yellow-green of morning sun low off the water of the inner harbor, remembering the fresh vernal odor of the incoming tide, and imagining the cunt smell she'd left on the fingers of his right hand even though he couldn't really smell it, going back for just one more whiff again and again, as if it were the most exotic perfume or the ultimate no-fault cocaine. He thought he'd see her again after that, but she disappeared. Somebody told him she took a job in San Diego.

At first his rambles were an idyll, but gradually the weekends stretched from Thursdays to Sundays. The drugs did something else, too. He didn't have words for it, but the image was of his walking-around body being offset from the center of himself. The drugs made him feel good when he didn't feel good, but then, sober, there were moments when he should've felt good and felt nothing. He was functional, showing up at the Historical Society four days a week, yet many other symptoms lurked.

The waterfront junkies could've recited them rote—the not shitting for a week, or the yawning gulf of terrible sickness he fell into the time Dr. Paulson took a vacation. With all his might the Mailman resisted, ignored, denied. The junkies—like tentacles of the old Turk's load—understood it was just a matter of time. Not that they gave a damn.

The Brain in the Jar

After the clams and Bloody Marys, Kelly began to feel chipper. He was needling Norbert, a die-hard Yankees fan, about the Amazin' Mets when the stool beside him scraped the sawdust floor and a pale face loomed through the underwater light.

"Lloyd. Is this an office visit?"

"I had some business in the area."

To Kelly, Lloyd Chamberlain was a man adrift. Blond, fey, and smooth, Lloyd was a trust funder from some wealthy New England family, supposedly working as an artist. But Lloyd had gotten into acid and contagious-looking splotches of paint, then speed and no paint at all. He was dealing now, not that he needed the money, and had replaced painting with talking, always talking, only occasionally about art. If there was a genetic predisposition to the low life, this poor bastard had it. Kelly pitied him, vaguely liked him, hoped he'd turn himself around, but saw nothing wrong with using him in the meantime. Lloyd was on the street a lot. Saw things. Knew people.

As far as Lloyd was concerned, it was Kelly who was the odd man out. Unless you actually *were* a narcotics agent or a jazz musician, you should *not* dress in shiny black shoes, dark sport coats, and skinny ties. Still, the private detective was a decent companion—stolid, a good listener. And he could handle himself.

Kelly finished his drink, and Lloyd proposed they mosey downtown. He and Helen were having people over that night and she wanted him out while she got the place together. The two of them could hang for a while, then Kelly could come over to his pad. That suited Kelly. Prior to the mess with the German he'd done a difficult divorce case—a lot of surveillance and not much sleep—and was now serious about laying low. An afternoon of moderate drinking followed by an evening of Chamberlain's arty and intellectual friends didn't sound strenuous. Plus, there would be Helen. Kelly had a thing for Lloyd's wife.

They had dark beers, hard cheese, and raw onions in the company of dozing cats and muttering geezers at a place in the Village. As the students began drifting in they moved west, toward Lloyd's "business," stopping at My Office on Hudson, a dingy railroad car of a joint with only two other customers. Lloyd and Kelly stood way down at the end, under the TV around the corner from the men's room, facing the front door, a distant rectangle of pearly light in the gloom. Kelly ordered two Schaefers.

Lloyd was in a pathologically chatty mood, even for him, probably because he was cranked. Kelly listened patiently. Finally he said, "There's something green stuck between your teeth."

Lloyd stopped talking, stared at the other man intently, then walked out of the bar. Kelly lit a cigarette and waited. Lloyd returned fifteen minutes later and pushed Kelly around the corner into the phone booth by the men's room, pulling a plasticene envelope of dirty white powder from his pocket. He made two minuscule piles of the stuff on the flap and held them up to his nose with one hand.

The thumb and slender ring finger of the other held the half-length of blue-and-white-striped soda straw and the index finger blocked the nostril as he sucked up one of the piles. Second pile in the other nostril. His back stiffened. He offered the envelope to Kelly.

Hitting the street again, they stopped at one more run-down gin mill for another toot, perfectly timed to catch the receding wave of the first, before heading across town to Lloyd's apartment. On the way, Lloyd told him about a lifer in the army, a platoon leader in 'Nam, who'd gotten all shot up. Which was when the helicopter came down, a big flying, stainless steel state-of-the-art operating room, and scooped him up. Just shoved the regular medevacs out of the way and sucked the mangled body up inside it and disappeared.

Kelly looked over at Lloyd, who caught the look and said, "No. I actually know this guy. I mean I know about the guy whose identity they stole and put him into. I read the b-book about what they're doing."

Something in his voice. "What're they doing, Lloyd?"

"They're looking for a fucking B-BRAIN." Flecks of white spittle dotted the corner of his mouth.

"Lloyd . . ."

"No. I read—I read the book and the fucking reports, too." Kelly let him talk.

A top secret government organization had been working on this, Lloyd went on, since the end of World War II. They'd put the finishing touches on the technology just in time for Vietnam, which was perfect. What they needed, apparently, was a brain. They thought they were going to have to use car crash victims in their experiments but now the war provided an endless supply of mangled bodies with heads intact. That stainless steel chopper would swoop down and get the poor bastard and then they'd take out his brain— Kelly experienced a jangling flashback to Norbert's hands on those clams—and keep it alive. Because what they needed was something to organize their computing devices.

"They've got all these Univacs running along, giant things, they fill up rooms. Some monitor electricity, some do the railroads and airlines. Some, they listen to telephone calls, see who's calling who. Some keep track of charge accounts. Not to mention the military stuff. The thing is, it's so much information that no machine can handle it. So they've been working on ways to wire human brains into the machines. Some are like traffic control, you know, switching devices, and some are like moles running through all this information for the Man."

Despite himself, Kelly got the picture. Computers the size of houses with wires to brains in jars at the bottom of a deep gray canyon of chemical nutrient. Hadn't there even been some movie?

"So they got this guy's brain, but they didn't get all the personality out."

"How do you know they got him, Lloyd?"

"He's been trying to fucking CONTACT me." It was almost a wail. Lloyd had been getting coded messages on his telephone and electric bills. They looked like gibberish. He couldn't figure them out. The poor bastard was on the ragged end of a weeklong speed run—couldn't tell the traffic buzz from the one in his head.

Lloyd heard the thought, the way they sometimes could on crank. "Fuck you, Kelly. I didn't say I b-believed it. I'm just laying it down the way I think about it. I think about it a lot. And how strange is it compared to all the other weird shit going on out there?"

Weird shit. That was for sure.

Daddy's Stash

The *foco*, their revolutionary cell, hung out at Gallagher's place on the Lower East Side. The living was communal and informal, but the lifestyle was highly politicized, an ongoing planning session involving the core group—Kevin, Gloria, Leo, and Juan. Lloyd Chamberlain came and went, usually delivering drugs, and Irene hovered at the fringes as legal consultant, scrupulously avoiding firsthand knowledge of their plots and schemes. They all had their own places in the city, but they might as well have lived at Kevin's, as much time as they spent there. Gloria slept with him regularly—at first. But as his head issues became apparent, she tailed off. He needed for her to be his "whore" or his "bitch" and that doggie-style thing was way too hung up. He was, she soon realized, damaged. A user, a hustler, a loser. For the rest: Leo lacked discipline, Lloyd was a drug addict, and poor Juan just wanted to be wherever Irene was.

Originally they'd bonded over their shared belief in the corruption and imminent failure of the establishment. All were certain that there were things they could do to hasten the inevitable end. The most radical group dedicated to this mission was a shadowy band of dedicated revolutionaries who called themselves the Motherfuckers. In the *foco* only Juan and Lloyd weren't Motherfucker dropouts, Gloria and Irene by choice, Leo and Kevin because of their "adventurism," which Kevin claimed was Motherese for having more brains than they—very unlikely in Gloria's view. They bounced him because, no matter what Kevin said, they recognized him as a liability.

As far as Gloria was concerned, the Mother commitment to violent overthrow of the established order was too limited, too inflexible—suicidal, really, which was what made it sexy. Kevin was obsessed with doing something to impress them, to show them they'd made a mistake about him. So he was always talking about spectacular schemes like kidnapping someone from Mundi Enterprises or blowing up government buildings.

At this moment, for example, he was coiled on the edge of his ratty couch, intense and crazy. Gloria, he announced, would dress in maternity clothes, padded big, like seven or eight months pregnant. She'd come into a station house in obvious distress and ask to use the ladies' room. Then she'd plant two sticks of dynamite hidden in the stuffing, along with a simple alarm clock detonator, behind the toilet or in the trash can.

Juan nodded eagerly, ready for anything. Leo was excited about doing something big with Kevin. Lloyd was off somewhere, but that was okay. No one really counted on him for anything except pot. Gloria contemplated walking around with dynamite taped to her, setting alarm clock detonators in a police station bathroom, while her accomplices waited, blocks away.

It was always the same pattern: Kevin concocting a bold scheme that involved someone else taking the risk. Not that it mattered. His plans never came to fruition. Irene would put her foot down, or Lloyd would show up with some acid and they'd all get distracted, or the idea would start to seem fatally flawed before it could be put into execution.

The inevitable flaw was they were scared. Especially Kevin. When you blew up buildings people got killed. Other people hunted you down. So they muddled along, Kevin ranting and scheming, Leo aping Kevin, Juan adoring Irene, and Irene and Gloria putting their efforts into funding and delivering legal aid for antiwar demonstrators and conscientious objectors, the only useful accomplishment of the *foco* to date.

Now this. Maternity bombs.

She'd been a fool to let Kevin know about Daddy's stash. Instead of figuring out how to get it—instead of helping her to get it—and fence it, and use the proceeds to start *focos* in major cities, greased with lawyers and funds, Kevin did nothing. Said nothing. Talked darkly of "the right time." Instead of seeking the advice and counsel of the group, he was using all the power and intimidation he could muster to get her to keep quiet, to keep it from them. Did he really believe she couldn't see through him? Did he imagine this dynamite business was going to distract her? Yet here he was tonight, working harder to sell it than she'd ever seen him.

"The pigs won't have a clue. We head north and into Syracuse —I've got people up there—and do it again. Other groups will see how easy it is. That's when things'll get interesting. We'll be the spark. And here's the kicker"—he glared around intently, trying to judge whether they were worthy conspirators—"I've got funding for this one. An old friend. A guy whose life I saved in jail. It's a long story, but"—he produced a fat wad of bills—"three grand. Enough to get us a set of wheels that can't be traced. Enough to set us up again somewhere else. This is going to *happen*, people, if we want it to. All I need is for you to tell me. Is this what we *want?*"

She could see it clearly now. It was all a diversion. The bastard intended to steal Daddy's stash for himself. That was what all that prying and digging had been about. Or he'd get some other people in, serious criminal types who knew how to maximize an asset. Whatever it was.

While Gloria stewed, the "whatever" waited in Richard Mundi's safe.

Helen and Kelly

There was a crowd at Lloyd and Helen's that night. Friends of Helen's with long dresses, armpit hair, sandals. A couple of brothers in wide-brimmed hats, bell-bottoms showing under long coats, studiously avoiding one another. A few cutting-edge radicals from the Motherfuckers, keeping regally to themselves, and another bunch of activists, Lloyd's buddies, who'd made their stand in the kitchen, as far away from the Motherfuckers as they could get, in company with various writers, drug addicts, actors, and a tight knot of what looked to be graduate assistants standing around the stove. Why did intellectuals always go to the kitchen?

The Chamberlains had the second floor of a building on the corner of Sixth, with a large central window onto Avenue B, and they'd knocked the walls out, so it was now a loft space. Most of the far wall, away from the stairs, was fronted by boards on sawhorses loaded with potluck food: loaves of homemade bread, salads, vegetable and grain stuff in heavy clay bowls. Kelly considered himself lucky to discover a tinfoil tray of chicken wings that someone had brought over from the local Chinese takeout. He nibbled for a while, had a beer. Lloyd gave him a handful of teeny little reds. He took a few and gave the rest to an anorexic blonde who definitely looked wigged. She smiled and said, "*Gaww*."

The pills went down and down, trying their hardest, but they still couldn't get him back on the wave. His brain kept trying to tell him who it thought he was.

He did slow circuits of the big room, getting a face here, a snatch of conversation there, passing easily in the crowd but stopping conversation when he stood with a group of three or four. Although he couldn't possibly have been a narc, his presence invariably elicited hostile silence. It was the shoes, mostly, as Lloyd had told him many times.

Lloyd, who'd opted to stay with the speed, did a couple of turns with Kelly, then started moving faster and faster, until he disappeared completely from view. Kelly found himself in the kitchen, standing near a group whose number had grown, the way a mob gathers around two guys fighting in the street.

In this case it was a linebacker-size dude with shoulder-length hair and a rakish mustache, and a lissome, very put-together girl—B-school or law firm—with a most beguiling way of wrinkling the corners of her eyes. It gave her a certain lightness of being, as if she were tuned in, underneath it all, to some cosmic joke.

What she was saying, however, was anything but funny. Kelly thought it might have been a lover's quarrel cloaking itself in political debate. The guy was invoking the grinding poverty of Guatemalan peasants, and she was saying, basically, fuck that. The realities of the post-scarcity economy proved they were never going to get theirs until the system changed.

"All the help you wish you could give them, Kevin, is just postponing the inevitable. And what do you think you could actually *do* down there, anyway? What have you done up here?"

Kelly sighed. A lovers' quarrel was at least more interesting, in some immediate way, than the Revolution. Then he glanced across the room and saw Helen standing by the refrigerator, a wineglass in her hand, smiling back at him. She was tall and slender, with straight hair, deep green eyes, ample breasts, and a slightly hysterical laugh, which he considered proof of the frustrated passion raging within her. She had a pouty mouth and a way of tilting her head so that her hair came partway over her face, making her seem vulnerable and already violated all at once. The beat-up dame. He was crazy for her.

They looked at each other for a long time, undressing in their minds. He approached. She tilted her head and stroked his lapel with the back of her long white hand.

"You seem so beautiful to me when I'm drunk," she said.

"I know," he replied. "You, too." Now he ran his hand along her slender shoulder, down her bare arm, snared her fingers with his. "Let's go up on the roof."

"No," she said, "We'd better not."

There was something wrong about her, and Kelly knew it was her husband's money. Ultimately Lloyd would wind up dead or in rehab, and she'd be widowed or divorced, and slide into what was left of his dough. All she had to do was sit there and watch, as his life went down the drain. It didn't make her seem like a very nice person, but it didn't cause Kelly to want her any less. His desire for her was just a habit, like smoking, that had been pleasurable at first. Now all it did was kill time at parties.

He went up to the roof and had a smoke.

All About Mundi Enterprises

"Jurgen Kramer thinks you're pretty good at what you do."

Richard Mundi's blond hair was turning white, and he combed it forward like Burton in *Cleopatra*. He must've been something in his prime—maybe five foot eight with thick square shoulders and the shortest arms Kelly had ever seen on a human. The hands were square, too. Stumpy strong fingers that looked like they could remove lug nuts without a wrench. Kelly figured the man had started as a truck driver. But he was old now and gone to seed. His belly ran from thighs to shoulders and his face was red, as if he had trouble with his blood pressure or was drinking a quart of whiskey a day.

Kelly had already been grilled by Mundi's bulldog, a tough-looking chunk of muscle by the name of Roth. He'd had to answer a lot of questions regarding his prior employers, his qualifications for this line of work, and the types of jobs he was willing to do. His memory was fairly well tapped out. He couldn't remember who Jurgen Kramer was.

Mundi Enterprises was on the thirtieth floor of the Tishman Building, the new one on Fifth Avenue, all glass and aluminum, with the big *666* lit up in red numbers on the top floor at night.

On the doorway to the office suite it said ME in gold leaf. Kelly wasn't rushing to judgment, but maybe Richard Mundi did make his money doing the devil's work. The man's clipped directness suggested loan-sharking, extortion, numbers, drugs, and prostitution. He could have been a made guy except that no Mafioso would ever hire a private dick. Kelly sat in one of the heavy leather office chairs, hat in his lap. Mundi stood like a fireplug in front of his desk.

"Who's Jurgen Kramer?"

Manhattan played an endless Warhol movie through the immense office windows. Mundi opened a file of papers, which, except for a telephone and an ashtray, was the only object marring the blank perfection of the vast mahogany surface of his desk. He extracted a business card from the file and handed it across. It was Kelly's card, with a name and phone number written on the back of it.

"Kramer works for a West German construction cartel. They wanted to get something going over here and they were looking at my company as a way in. Kramer was their rep. Apparently you hauled his ass out of a difficult situation."

Past tense. The deal must've fallen through. Remembering the German made Kelly's ankle throb.

"Kramer needs a brain, Mr. Mundi, not a PI."

"Forget about him. He told me about you, is all, when I inquired about his broken nose. Said you could handle yourself. As it happened I needed to hire someone and he gave me your card."

Kelly eyed the file. "Everyone's got needs. What are yours, exactly?"

"I'm concerned about my daughter." He paused, looked at the ceiling. This was difficult for him. "Worried about her future."

Kelly didn't say anything. He extended his feet and leaned back in the chair. His hat was in his lap and his hands were clasped over his belly. He was going to wait until Mundi cut the shit. If that didn't happen, he was going to say he didn't think he could help and walk toward the door.

Mundi got the message right away. "All right. Here's the deal. My daughter's been running around with a creep named Kevin Gallagher. I don't know who the fuck he thinks he is, but he's trouble. Some kinda Communist, or revolutionary, supposedly. A bad influence."

"I'm not a leg-breaker, Mr. Mundi."

"Oh yes, you are. But that's not the issue here. I just want you to tail Gallagher and my daughter. I want to know what they're up to."

"Him or your daughter?"

"Him. But as near as I can tell she's with him all the time."

"So I spy on your daughter and her boyfriend. Where does that get us?"

"Well, he's some kind of professional agitator. Already been arrested a couple of times. I'm sure the Feds'd love to put him away."

Kelly looked through the glass wall behind Mundi, where the north tower of the World Trade Center was clawing the sky like Ronan emerging from his egg. "You've got a big operation here, Mr. Mundi. Don't you have people who could take care of this for you?"

Mundi shook his head. "I've got the best. But this'll tell you something about my daughter. A few years ago, the summer after she graduated college, she was doing some kinda poverty program down south. And I sent my guys down to keep an eye on her, and all that happened was, she made them right away. And they came back and said, 'Boss, this is a waste of time. Your daughter don't need us.'" He began fidgeting with the file. "That's the kind of kid she is, see? Smart. Independent."

"Only child?"

"Yeah, why?"

"How old is she?"

"Twenty-six."

"Don't you think she's old enough to make her own bad decisions?"

"You don't understand. She's going to be running this company someday. She's the future, and the future is pretty damned soon. This Gallagher is turning her against me. Ever since she started going around with him—no, even before—it's been different. First, it was poverty and civil rights. That wasn't so bad, even if it was unrealistic. Then it was the war. We had plenty of arguments, believe me, but I could still respect her position. She just hasn't seen enough, doesn't understand how things work."

Kelly could imagine the arguments. Stubborn old man, headstrong rich girl. This guy had been through the Depression and World War II. He'd seen the system and he trusted it. All his kid could see was the bullshit, the hypocrisy.

"She's an idealist. Maybe that's not so bad."

"That's beside the point, dammit. She's turned into a fanatic about what she refers to as moral issues. We do construction and real estate, see? Nothing to do with the government. But ever since this Gallagher's gotten hold of her, she's thinking of this company— our company—as part of the system. Part of the problem. Now it's the people's struggle. Fuckin' revolution."

Mundi stopped, in distress.

"What does her mother think of all this?"

"My wife died ten years ago."

"I'm sorry to hear that. What's your daughter's name?"

"Gloria. This was supposed to be her second year of law school. Columbia. She's a smart one, I'm telling you. But that's in the shitter now. This Gallagher's stolen her mind."

In Kelly's view, it was never a good idea for men like Richard Mundi to show pain. It was blood in the water. Kelly nodded respectfully, helping bring him down a little.

"I think I understand what you mean."

"Anyway, she knows who my people are. She'd be furious if she found out I was . . ."

Kelly thought he could see it pretty clearly. It wasn't Gloria. It wasn't Gallagher, either. This was some kind of come-on. Mundi wanted him around for some obscure reason—something he wasn't owning up to—and that captured Kelly's interest. He gave a sympathetic nod.

"So it's really about this Gallagher."

"I just want her to see the truth about the people she's running with."

"Something messy."

"I didn't say that."

"But that's the way you'd like it."

"All right, goddamn it. I don't care what it is. I want him gone. You interested in the job or not?"

"All I can promise you is information. Anything else, we'll just have to see what happens. And it'll cost you a hundred a day plus expenses."

Mundi reached in his pocket and came out with a dainty, banded stack of bills. A grand, Kelly guessed. He took a white envelope from the file folder, slipped the bills inside, placed it in the file, and handed the whole thing to Kelly.

"Do your job and there's more."

Kelly took it from him, stared at the shape of the empty desk, was reminded suddenly of a coffin, of the dead Mrs. Mundi, of this guy trying to steer an only child into adulthood. Misreading Kelly's silent stare as a comment on the emptiness of his desk, Mundi broke into his reverie. "I move people, Kelly. Not paper."

Kelly nodded, rose. "I'll look this stuff over. If I think I can help I'll send you a weekly report with consultation any time you ask for it. If the job's not for me, you'll get the money back tomorrow."

But that was just client talk. The world had already redefined itself around Mundi's problem. Kelly's job now was to figure out what his new employer's problem really was, and how to solve it if it could be solved, and how to stay unharmed while doing so, in a manner that resulted in his being further paid cash money or otherwise rewarded. Kelly was happiest absorbed like this.

He walked past his own office and on to Sammy's, thinking of the wad in the white envelope, imagining what kind of information the money might buy. He didn't want to look in the folder yet. He didn't want details about the girl and her boyfriend and the father and dead mother. He just wanted to move them around, for now, into the classic configurations.

Little hunks of mind cheese, like a man setting himself up for heartbreak by forcing his rebellious daughter into a role she didn't want. A spoiled, willful girl determined to escape her domineering father. A predatory boyfriend who knew how to work his meal ticket. And vaguely—the late Mrs. Mundi. His instinct told him *she* could be the key to all this.

He'd have to figure out her story to get to the bottom of Mundi's bullshit, which would mean having Jarkey tail Gloria, which was fine. That was how he'd do it.

The clams arrived, Bloody Mary standing tall behind them.

Good Old Julie

Julius Roth had a shiny balding head, a thick neck, and slabs of torso that rippled beneath his short-sleeved white shirt. He projected the genial physicality of a football player who'd taken up accountancy and he reinforced the impression by keeping a mechanical pencil in his breast pocket.

Richard Mundi had discovered Roth during the postwar years when he, Jimmy Murchison and Harlan Kraft, were doing suburban developments on Long Island. The sprawl was moving unstoppably across Nassau County and he and his partners were getting very rich buying farmland cheap and turning it into "affordable housing"— acres of tacky boxes with names like Seaview Heights. Julius Roth, really just a kid then, was one of Murchison's project managers and he stood out from the hard, greedy crowd of low-level bosses because he had an uncanny ability to make men work. Itinerant framers, Canuck wallboard guys, burned-out GI electricians, it didn't matter. Roth had his crews running like drill teams. He was as tough as any, but he was smart with people, too, and Mundi recognized he was bound for bigger things. So he took him on as a protégé and Roth blossomed. Mundi then moved him over to the Newark operation and watched him work his way to the top of the heap, overseeing the squads of snoops, mules, and goons in that branch of the enterprise. It turned out to have been a brilliant move.

Along with his nascent administrative skills, Roth demonstrated a knack for real estate. As the Long Island action dried up, he began acquiring distressed properties in the greater Newark area on behalf of Mundi Enterprises. He was able to squeeze value out of these tenements, small businesses, and defunct industrial sites by recycling them for use by immigrants and African-American entrepreneurs. Over the years he'd turned Newark into the company's sole profit source, and now he answered only to Mundi, having risen above Seamster and Mossman, displacing Murchison and Kraft in the chain of command.

At the moment he was briefing his boss on a troubling occurrence over in Jersey. Two of their offices, the one on Ferry Street and the one down on Hillside Avenue, had been tossed. In broad daylight. No doubt about it being Mob guys, either. They'd barged in, slapped people around, emptied drawers, and turned over desks, just the way they'd come around trying to intimidate some business, trying to muscle in. Except it wasn't a shakedown.

"They're letting you know that *they* know you've got their stuff," Roth told his boss.

"It's a bluff."

"Call it that. But it's also a reasonable deduction. First, they wait for the shit to show up on the streets. When that doesn't happen, they start looking around for someone smart enough to sit them out. They have to figure out the whole operation and who's running it. When they get all that, then they start to squeeze."

"Fuck them."

"You don't want to get into it with those guys."

"They got no proof of anything. Seamster took care of that at street level. There's no fuckin' way they can connect us. They're just shaking trees, waiting for something to fall out."

"Maybe. But supposing they tried everyone else and you're the last one left? They're gonna shake pretty damned hard."

"So I'm supposed to wrap it in a baby blanket and leave it outside their door?"

"Look, Boss, we should've sold that shit the day we found it. Or even better, just handed it back to DiNoto. He would've treated us right. Now it's just a matter of time before he's on to us, if he isn't already. All I'm saying is, you need to figure out how to get the stuff back to them or you'll have a real problem."

Mundi swiveled his chair around and stared through the window into brown gloom. He didn't want to figure anything out. He needed a rest. But he wasn't going to get one anytime soon.

For the past ten days Manhattan had been trapped under a bubble of cold air, breathing and rebreathing its own gasses. Such things occasionally happened in the summer. The papers called it a temperature inversion. Mundi guessed the air was toxic by this time. It certainly looked like it could kill you.

His chest felt constricted. It was all polluted. Everything. From some primal leak. The cosmic sump pump on the long-forgotten universal construction site, coughing out vile ooze, *ka-thunk, splat,* as the great wheel went around, probing the same cesspool over and over. A dead wife, a daughter who was breaking his heart, and a business that was going under. Now Roth was pressing him for an answer to the latest problem. What the fuck did Roth know about problems?

The whole operation was in the tank, had been for years. They'd long since run out of gullible Long Island farmers, and the Newark riots had devastated their underinsured or uninsured properties there. To make matters worse, the Germans—who initially seemed very interested in a major deal for Newark—had backed out, frightened by the uprising of *die Schwartzen*. Didn't even ask to look at the books, which had been Mundi's greatest dread prior to the riots.

Now Roth wanted him to go crawling to DiNoto, begging for a break. Fuck that. All Roth cared about was keeping Mundi Enterprises alive so that he'd have a job. He'd been a good soldier, Mundi would never say otherwise. Back in the old days he'd even been a creative force. But lately he was just on the tit like everybody else. Well, that act was getting old. It was time to lose him. It was time to fold the whole fucking outfit.

The more he thought about it, the more it made sense to shut Mundi Enterprises down. Gloria didn't want any part of the company, so what point was there trying to save it? For that matter, in trying to win her back, trying to convince her of anything? She'd already made her choices.

It was damned sad, he saw now, because the choice had been his. He'd always been too busy, too distracted to put in any real time with her. There'd always been reasons. When Gloria was an infant he told himself he'd be able to relate to her better when she could talk. When she learned to talk he realized the things he had to say were too serious for a little girl, so he decided to wait. Then her mother's health problems came to dominate everything and there never seemed to be the right moment. Now his daughter was full-grown, and the two of them had no language, no experience, nothing in common. Hell, Roth had been more of a father to her than he.

This line of thought was almost immediately displaced by a whole scrapbook of images of Gloria's sullen face, ages one to twenty-six, by memory flashes of her tantrums, of her sidelong glimpses of intense loathing—when all he'd done was love her, his only child, as completely as he could. He'd provided her with the best life he could—including a high-class education—and the fact that she'd chosen to throw it back in his face was her decision, not his. It was probably the fucking education that put the nail in the coffin. Big mistake.

Thinking about Gloria in this way caused him to remember the detective, Kelly. Suddenly, Mundi's depression and self-pity were enhanced by a pang of mortal embarrassment. What was he doing, hiring a dick—laying out his troubles to a complete stranger? It had been a desperate, sentimental gesture and would only make things worse with Gloria. He'd have to whack Kelly, too.

Not literally, of course. Just that it was time to cut and run. And if Julie thought those drugs were going back to DiNoto, he had another think coming. That load of heroin, purring contentedly in the safe across the room, was going to be his ticket out.

Roth looked at the back of Mundi's chair and reflected on the shame of it all. Instead of trimming their operation and moving it to Newark, they were running on fumes and Mundi's ego. Coughing up thousands for a fancy midtown office, feeding on themselves. Instead of parlaying their lucky find into some small advantage with the Mob—something that could be useful to the operation in Newark— Mundi was going to try to sell it out from under them. Roth could practically hear the old man's brain laboring through its plan. The poor guy actually thought he'd be able to take the money and run.

The whole scenario distressed Roth. He remembered what he'd loved about Richard Mundi, how exciting it had been when the two of them were lean and hungry and on the make. There was nothing Roth wouldn't have done for him back then. And, in fact, he'd done *most* of it—with a feral sense of purpose and not the slightest twinge of conscience. But as age overtook Mundi, he began backing himself too frequently into corners. Roth's talents got sucked up into continual damage control—stuff that was unpredictable, potentially dangerous, aggravating. He wasn't having fun anymore.

The worst of it was, he knew instinctively that feeling this way made him vulnerable. Just like on the football field. If he couldn't do the job with absolute energy and commitment, he was going to get hurt.

When he thought of the situation in those terms it boiled down to a choice between Mundi and himself, and that was no choice at all. He'd had a wonderful run, but it was over now. That thing with Smoot had been the final straw.

The chair swiveled back around and Mundi regarded Roth. What he saw was a slightly anxious man, but one still ready to deal with the situation in whatever way Mundi thought necessary. Just not ready to figure this thing out by himself. Never ready to take charge, to run the show. Roth would never be anything but a glorified gofer. Mundi sighed, gathered himself, slapped his thick palms on the desk.

"All right, Julie. You shut things down in Newark. Send everybody home for a week."

"Boss, if you take that smack they'll kill you."

Mundi looked at him, said nothing.

Roth considered walking out right then, but it didn't feel right. So for the fifth time that week, he outlined his plan whereby Mundi Enterprises would go into partnership with DiNoto, returning the heroin and offering the shell of their company as a money-laundering apparatus for DiNoto's drug money.

Mundi listened, as he had the first four times, nodding at all the right places. But Roth understood.

"I hear you, Julie. I just don't want anyone stepping on his pecker over there in Newark until we get this thing resolved."

"Okay. Then maybe you could take a little break yourself, huh?"

"What do you mean?"

"I dunno. When was the last time you played a round of golf? You look a little tired, is all." In fact, he looked like shit.

"Good old Julie." Mundi regarded him with paternal benevolence, thinking all the while, *I'm gonna whack this guy.*

Roth gave him a fond smile. *I'm outta here,* he thought.

Ilda

It all came apart for the Mailman that July. Then it came back together.

Having been looped on codeine for days and locked in utter despair for months, he woke one morning wanting heroin more than he'd ever wanted anything in his life. The shit had been abundant all spring and he'd been skin-popping with a comical, growling, scoundrel named Langer. Now supplies had dried up and the Mailman found himself with a gut-gnawing yen for more. Langer wisecracked about getting his health back on a "juice and herbs" diet—booze and grass—but it was no joke to the Mailman. So far, he'd been able to maintain appearances. But he was regularly showing up for work stoned, and he knew he'd fuck something up sooner or later. Even worse, he was already spending his pension check every month on drugs. He had a few thousand dollars remaining in what he referred to as his "retirement fund," but he knew how long that would last once he started tapping it. Then there'd be nothing left but auto theft, B and E, and who knew what forms of degradation.

Lying there in his sweaty puddle of anguish and need, he realized a couple of other things. He realized that he had to get some smack, and he realized that if he did his life would be over. The cancer hadn't killed him, but it had opened a door. He'd gone in, and it had been the wrong door. He'd gotten locked in a room where there was nothing but the drugs. He'd been fighting that realization for years; suddenly, this particular morning, the battle seemed over.

The old Turk's load was whispering in his ear, all the way from Manhattan. But the Mailman still had his pride, and he had the powerful negative example of Langer with which to resist its blandishments. He was damned if he'd turn into a fucking junkie.

He decided to kill himself.

An overdose would be the simplest way but—no surprise, actually—he discovered on consulting his meds that he had only three Demerols left. He lit out for Dr. Paulson's, found him in, wrote a desperate note testifying to the intensity of his pain and his fears that the cancer had returned, received a prescription as expected, and, once he was back in his car and secure in the knowledge that more awaited, crushed his last three pills and dumped the acrid powder onto his tongue. He was walking out of the pharmacy with a new bottle when they hit, more like a hum than a buzz.

He sat in his car in the parking lot and thought about taking the pills down to Stage Fort Park and making himself comfortable under a tree with a bottle of wine at the edge of Half Moon Beach—looking across the harbor at that lovely view of the city—and grinding them up into the wine. He was sure he could get them all down before he passed out. Then it occurred to him that he might get discovered. What if they hauled his sorry-ass wannabe corpse to the emergency room in time to save him? The only sure way would be to lock himself in his apartment. Nobody would miss him. Nobody would find him till the stench tipped them off. But the thought of fouling his apartment in that manner disgusted him—sometimes the simplest things got so fucking complicated. Ilda would smell him and she'd be stuck with discovering him. The thought of Ilda brought on an unexpected recollection.

When he'd first moved into his basement the backyard had been a trash-strewn mess. Over the years, working a little at a time, he'd made it into a clear grassy area with a modest garden of tomato plants, squash, and greens. He wasn't an avid gardener, had no interest in flowers, but the rhythms of turning the soil in the spring and watering each evening comforted him. Besides, he really liked tomatoes. After several years Mr. Menezes, up on the second floor, erected a clothesline out there for his wife who, after several more years, became sufficiently unafraid of the Mailman to hang her wash out while he was in the yard reading the newspaper in his rusty lawn chair. She'd finish, pat her hands into her apron, and stand with him in the sun for a few minutes, smiling silently, since she spoke no English. When he lost his voice they were even.

After his operation the only one who could get a sound out of him was Ilda, the Menezes' daughter, who'd been born about the time of the clothesline, and probably had been the cause of its erection. She was dark and beautiful and fearless from the first, and liked to play with the Mailman on the days he sat in the yard. She'd just started school when he got the operation, and she questioned him relentlessly, wanting to see the blowhole and the rest of the scar—the upper portion of it was quite visible, despite the Mailman's post–post office beard—to know if it had hurt, and to get him to demonstrate for her, over and over, how he was learning to replicate speech by manipulating a prolonged burp. She taught him the Portuguese names for all the vegetables in his garden and made him repeat them in burp-talk, until even in the Mailman's mind kale was no longer kale but *coivsch*.

Being the only fluent English speaker in her family, Ilda had some gaps. Once, after her mother had hung out the wash, and the three of them were in the backyard, she pointed to a bedsheet hanging on the line and asked, "What's that?" The Mailman, disarmed by the question, made a confused face. Ilda went over and touched the sheet and said in perfectly unaccented American, "This. What's its name? How do you call it in English?" And he realized it was a word she'd heard around the house in Portuguese but not in English in her first grade classroom. Burping "sheet," however, was a chore. She knew it couldn't be "shit" and was hung up on "cheat" for quite a while before she got it right. This was the occasion of considerable laughter; even Mrs. Menezes joined in.

The thought of Ilda and her laugh mixed with the steadying Demerol hit and bumped him off his suicidal groove. He drove from the pharmacy to work, completed his morning chores there, went up to the library, opened the scrapbook of newspaper clippings he'd been indexing, and just sat in front of it, feeling the pill bottle in his pants pocket, considering how close he'd come, how close he still was.

Then, even more unexpectedly—because this time there wasn't anything as remotely plausible as Ilda to account for it—he broke out of the room he'd been trapped in since his operation, and out of the house that had confined him all his life. It was a giddy tumble and it landed him in the midst of a new world, a new grand scheme. Sitting there in the dusty old library, the light was suddenly different. He drew a deep breath and the air rasping in through his blowhole seemed fresher and cleaner than any air ever had.

The Sound of Money

Kelly returned to his office to find his secretary slouched in front of a typewriter.

"Cheer up, Gorgeous. We've got a job!"

"Fuck you, Kelly."

Harry Jarkey was not gorgeous. He was a young, mule-faced investigative journalist who'd lost what he thought was going to be his career, as well as his marriage, when the *Herald Tribune* went under. Now he freelanced wherever he could, and used Kelly's office as his own. This was fine with Kelly, who felt he ought to have a secretary but never had enough cases for one. The tidy stacks of documents representing Jarkey's writing projects looked like the sort of paperwork a busy detective agency ought to generate. And Jarkey was, after all, a highly trained snoop. He occasionally did work for Kelly. It paid better and was more interesting than writing articles on adulterated dairy products for *Newsday*.

In exchange for his use of the office, Jarkey was required to keep track of Kelly's paperwork. That part was a snap. A brainless brunette with an hourglass figure could have done it. Nor did it bother him that, despite the fact he was not a brunette, Kelly insisted on calling him Gorgeous when he was in a good mood. Jarkey could tolerate the stale joke well enough. It was the glassy-eyed, post-hangover chipperness that drove him up a wall. The detective, perhaps a dozen years older than Jarkey, was something of a father figure. Jarkey couldn't help but view him with both respect and disdain.

Kelly had come in whistling, still wearing his hat, stinking of aftershave. He'd just made some easy money, or was about to make some easy money, or even *thought* he was about to make some easy money as a private detective. He'd be insufferable now.

In Jarkey's jaundiced view Kelly, rather than being a hard-boiled hero, was multiply addicted and delusional. Kelly himself would have agreed with that diagnosis. Everyone was addicted to something, and delusion was as necessary to life as oxygen.

Kelly dropped Richard Mundi's file in front of Jarkey, fetched a bottle and two glasses from his desk drawer, spread out the photos and information on Kevin Gallagher and Gloria, and began recapitulating his conversation with Mundi.

"This could be a sweet job, Jark. No heavy lifting. We give him a complete rundown on the lovebirds. Maybe we catch Gallagher actually breaking the law, maybe not. After a while we'll plant an ounce of grass in his pad and call the cops. He'll know he's gonna get fucked, so he'll jump bail and disappear. End of problem for Richard Mundi. The girl mopes around for a while, then goes back to law school."

"You're living in Fantasy Land, Kelly. Anyway, there's something else going on here. There always is."

Kelly pushed his hat back on his head, a move he'd learned from Darren McGavin's TV portrayal of Mike Hammer, and shrugged.

They inspected the photos. Gallagher, haranguing a crowd on the Columbia campus, was a good-looking guy with a thick mustache. Gloria looked mildly pretty all prepped up in her college graduation picture, a little more mature in glasses, a sweater, skirt, and pearls, standing next to her father in front of a Christmas tree. She reminded Kelly of someone, but he couldn't get a handle on whom.

Mundi had taken the trouble to obtain a copy of Gallagher's rap sheet. Six months' incarceration three years before, then nothing much, really, except trespassing and disorderly conduct—civil rights beefs—culminating in his recent arrest at an antiwar rally. The two men agreed he had the look of a committed opportunist. But he did have a record, which Kelly thought would make their job easier. He was feeling good about their prospects. Jarkey was not.

"You think this is going to be a snap. You're wrong. I happen to know for a fact that Richard Mundi is a sizeable operator. You get caught between him and Gallagher, it's likely to be uncomfortable. Furthermore, if it really is a family situation, it's twisted up in a different way. Complexity you'll never sort out."

At that moment Kelly recalled his recent, frustrating encounter with Helen Chamberlain. "Harry, I just remembered something. I know these two. I saw them both at a party at Lloyd Chamberlain's place the other night. And you know what they were doing? They were arguing about the fucking revolution! They're just babies. They don't have a clue."

This elicited a derisive snort from Jarkey. "I still don't like it. There's nothing in it but trouble."

"That, and a cool thousand." Kelly pulled the wad out of the envelope and fanned it in his face. "On account. C'mon, Jark. Can't you hear that money talking?"

Jarkey pushed his glasses back up his nose and blinked. "I can hear it. I'm just not sure what it's saying."

Jimmy, Richie, and Harlan

Across town Richard Mundi was having a private, high-level meeting with his partners, Jimmy Murchison and Harlan Kraft. They'd ordered in from Ruby's and were sitting around his desk eating pastrami sandwiches and talking, just like old times—except it seemed to Mundi more like feeding hour at the nursing home.

Murchison had gotten white and gaunt, like a starving Frankenstein, the flesh pulled back from his face. It had to be the Big C, though Jimmy didn't talk about it. Maybe they weren't telling him, but still. As for Kraft, Mundi'd had to drag him kicking and screaming off the golf course, all wizened, a little lizard with hooded eyes.

Mundi now had a plan, simple and direct. He'd pitch Roth's scheme about going into partnership with DiNoto. Murchison and Kraft, of course, would rubber-stamp it. Then the three would call Roth in and tell him to start the negotiations. Murchison would go back to bed, Kraft would go back to the links, and while Roth bounded off like a golden retriever—or as much like a golden retriever as a Jewish thug could be—Mundi would off-load the drugs to a guy he'd already lined up, grab some cash in return, and hop on a plane. He'd work the deal so fast, it'd make their heads spin. And if Julie or Jimmy or Harlan got caught in the blowback, tough shit. Maybe it'd wake them up.

After the usual preliminaries about Jimmy's grandchildren and Harlan's short game, Mundi got around to explaining how they'd happened to come into some valuable contraband and that soon the owners would be applying for its return.

"So give it back," coughed Murchison.

Mundi allowed as how that sounded like the sensible thing to do, except there were complications. As they all knew, the corporation was belly-up. Cash flow was zip because there were no new jobs, no acquisitions. They were consuming themselves in leases, fees, taxes, financing costs. Not to mention salaries.

Kraft wiggled in his seat. "Come off it, Richie. We all oughta be on Social and you know it. We've had a good dance for thirty years, made our money. But now this thing is dead meat around our necks. We're too old for this shit."

"The hell you say."

"Harlan's right, Rich. Look at that last deal. A couple more like it and we'll be in the poorhouse."

That was the Weehawken Mills project. Mundi Enterprises had gone into partnership with a developer who planned to turn a half-mile of Newark mill buildings into apartments. They'd raised their share by refinancing their Long Island properties. In the end they were undercapitalized. Real estate took a dip, rates went up, the banks came calling, and they lost the project to the marketing company. Assholes in BMWs with cashmere sweaters tied around their necks. It had been Mundi's play, for the most part, and it had cost him and his partners a lot.

There was little else to say about the episode. Kraft said it for him, as gently as he could. "Times are different now, Richie. Let's cash in our chips."

"Everything is leveraged up to the gills. We'd take a bath."

"So what are we going to do, live off this missing dope of yours? It *is* dope, isn't it?"

"It's heroin. It'd get us millions on the street right now." He waited for the number to take effect, to head their thoughts in the right direction. "But we're not gonna sell it ourselves. We'll use it as earnest money. Roth has a scheme worked out where he thinks we could turn this contraband into a more or less permanent arrangement. The original owners have a lot of free cash they're looking to place. Roth thinks they could be persuaded to see Mundi Enterprises as a gold mine of unrealized write-offs, bad debts, depreciations, and similar accounting bullshit. All we need is to pitch it the right way to the right people. We return the merchandise we've been safeguarding for them and they buy an interest in our construction operation, with periodic payments for maintenance, depreciation, whatever. We provide them with a legitimate business with a real track record and they boost our cash flow in return. After a few years we've paid our nut down and property values go back up. By then the government will be sending millions in grants to prop Newark back on its feet. Urban renewal in the worst of the slums. You know what that means?"

No response.

"It means we'll be selling Newark to the Feds! Isn't it sweet? That's when we clear out, Jimmy."

The color rose in Murchison's cheeks, but it didn't make him look much better. "Launder money for the fucking Mafia? Rich, have you lost your marbles?"

"It's twenty pounds of heroin, Jimmy! You wanna sell it yourself?"

Murchison and Kraft stared at him as if he'd gone mad. They were fossils, he thought sadly. They'd been useless for years. What was the point of even talking to them, except about old times?

Goodnight, Irene

Down at Kevin's they were trying to organize some street theater for a high school in the Bronx. Juan's cousin was a sophomore there, and that was how they found out that an army recruiter was scheduled to give the student body a lecture about Vietnam. The idea was to dress in clown suits and run through the halls distributing water balloons, squirt guns filled with blood-red food coloring, antiwar leaflets, and general mayhem. They knew a certain number of students would respond, helping spread the chaos, thus making the event a revolutionary teaching exercise. Juan went in with the cousin one day and got a layout of the building. They'd already decided who would enter which doors. Then they hit a problem.

The assembly was scheduled for nine a.m. If they waited until after it started, there wouldn't be any students in the hallways to catch the riot. On the other hand, if they launched their onslaught before the assembly began, they'd probably be ejected before the army guy took the stage, which would defeat one of the major purposes of the event, which was to stand at the back of the auditorium in their clown suits making a ruckus with New Year's Eve noise-makers while he was trying to speak.

They broke for a joint, giving Kevin the opening to start in again on his dynamite scheme. It was the moment Gloria was waiting for. She had it all planned out. She'd let him talk, then dissect the idea, showing how ludicrous it was. However, the more Kevin talked, the more annoyed she became, until finally she was so angry, she couldn't have dissected anything, except maybe him. She couldn't even shout. She hissed instead.

"Do you seriously expect anyone to carry dynamite into a police station while you sit on your fat ass two blocks away? You couldn't even get one of your twelve-year-old Chicana groupies down the street to pull a stunt like that. You're full of shit, Kevin. Your plan is full of shit."

Gallagher, sensing unusual danger in this attack, would not meet her eyes. He shot a "what a bitch" appeal to the other three men. Leo nodded. But Juan said, "You've been on this one all week, man. It's not going to fly. Give it a rest."

Lloyd, who'd just delivered an ounce of Acapulco Gold to Gloria, was standing on the other side of Gallagher's big front room, about to make his exit. He'd been cranked out, doing deliveries for two days, and still had a few more people to see. After that he was planning to tone it down a little, mellow out. He surveyed the scene with a judicious air and delivered his parting benediction. "You *both* need to take a break. I don't know what's wrong with you two, but everything's personal all of a sudden. You're creating an atmosphere that is not conducive to optimum results."

Kevin called him a bourgeois asshole. Gloria freaked. She went into the kitchen, gathered up the folders regarding pending trials that had accumulated on the table, marched through the front room with her eyes brimming, and pushed past Lloyd into the street. She felt like her brain was about to explode.

The journey up to 116th Street calmed her, and she thought she'd gotten it pretty much back together. But the instant she stepped into the office Irene looked up from her desk and said, "Gloria! What's the matter?"

"That jerk . . ." It was all jammed up, same as back at Kevin's. She dropped the folders on the desk and slumped disconsolately on the couch.

Irene came and sat beside her, gave her a hug and a reassuring pat. "Just start with one piece and tell it. The rest will come. Then you'll feel better."

So she started with the dynamite business, Irene watching her, smiling, listening. And by the time she got to the part about realizing that Kevin was manipulating her, Gloria realized she *did* feel better, except for one confusing thing.

"I just don't understand myself. Why couldn't I call Kevin out in front of the others? He's such a rat. But I just froze. And my father . . . first I couldn't stand him, and now I don't care. I don't have any feelings for him at all. It freaks me out."

"Gloria, I wish you could hear yourself."

"What do you mean?"

"What you're talking about is the way people *expect* you to react. It's like a big signal getting broadcasted all the time. Not in a paranoid way, it's just what happens in society, in the world. You're freaking out because you don't think or feel the way the world expects you to think or feel. But that's not a bad thing. It means you have your own thoughts and feelings. You have to trust them. You've probably got Kevin and your father and . . . *everything* figured out already and you don't even realize it. Just relax. Trust yourself."

They talked on in this manner, and Gloria was surprised and happy to discover the dreadful weight lifting from her shoulders. Could it be this simple? Was it possible that Irene was able to dispel her misery with just a few words? "How did you do that?"

"It's not me, honey. It's you."

Gloria looked at her friend's lovely face, trusted it, trusted herself, kissed it.

Irene returned the kiss. Gloria kissed her again. Irene's tongue sought her lips, parted them. Her long gentle hand had come around to the side of Gloria's breast. All tongues then, tender hands, soft breasts, slick dark moistness, tang of Irene's perspiration. Slow stroking, pressure and yielding, and Irene's vast, deep rush, right there on the couch in her office, as if it were any other business they'd transacted over the past two years.

Their lovemaking had exactly that likeness, with Irene's fingers working her just so, tongue on nipple completing the circuit that slid her so far into orgasm that she lost track of everything except the awareness that they were simply getting something done between them, as they always had, something fun and exciting and good for the world.

She could tell it was exactly that because when it was over— though it would never *really* be over, would it?—and Irene was splayed there on the couch, slender arms and legs in every direction, saying "Whew!" again and again—when it was over it wasn't like after Kevin or any man she'd ever been with, because even the best carried a vibe of possession or conquest, no matter how sweet or gentle. But not Irene, whom she loved, and would happily fuck again, anytime—or not—and with whom she would never have an affair, or be the partner of, because that wasn't what it was about.

It was the culmination of an evolving transaction during which, somehow, Irene had given Gloria her self, and in so doing had opened the world to her. The way Gloria would repay Irene would be to give that same thing to someone else, someday, not necessarily in Irene's way, but in her own. She saw all that in one instant, as if the world had opened up before her, and she was the first woman upon it, to see what she could make of it herself. That's what she saw. All at once.

And she said, "Whew."

Take the E Train

Two of Mundi's crisp C-notes settled Harry Jarkey's doubts, temporarily. Kelly, riding his hunch, had convinced him that the first thing to do was dig up background on Agnes Mundi. So Jarkey called Genzlinger at the *Times* and spent several hours that night in their morgue assembling a detailed report on Mundi's dead wife. The next day he handed the stack of photostatted clippings to Kelly, who accepted them with a serious, distracted air, undoubtedly hungover again. It was just about perfect, Jarkey thought. I go after the girl and her boyfriend while he stakes out a dead woman.

Kelly fished through his pockets to no avail, glanced at the empty hook on the wall behind his chair, then rummaged through his desk drawers. He found a .38 police special; half a book of five-cent stamps; a jar of Tang; a jar of instant coffee (both unopened); a bottle of aspirin, which he placed on top of the desk; a *Playboy* magazine; a pint of Wilson "That's All" blended whiskey; a pair of argyle socks; and a box of shells for the .38. He was beginning to get seriously interested in this excavation when Jarkey interrupted him.

"They're probably at the lot. With the car. Didn't you start leaving the keys at the lot?"

"I know there's an extra set around here somewhere."

"Well, while you look for them, I'll get the car and stake out the girl's place, do a tail, see what kind of routine she's got."

"Right," Kelly said. "And the camera." He began looking around the room again.

"In the car. The trunk. Remember?"

How did this man survive?

Kelly had a black '65 Fairlane, which he kept in a lot on the West Side. He liked it because it was inconspicuous in a crowd, perfect for tails, and could be mistaken for a cop car in the right circumstances. Jarkey liked it because Kelly hardly ever drove it, which made it, in effect, Jarkey's vehicle. He kept it cleaned and gassed and oiled and used it whenever he landed a freelance assignment that took him out to the Island or upstate. Late that afternoon he got a thermos from home and went down the street for coffee, sandwiches, film, and the day's papers. Then he took a cab to the lot, retrieved the car, drove down to Bank Street, and circled the block until nearly dark, when a space opened up a few doors from Gloria's apartment. A parking place was always the hardest part.

Beneath his crabby exterior, Jarkey was a gentle, thoughtful man. He'd fallen hopelessly in love with a selfish Julie Christie look-alike who didn't deserve him and who dumped him the moment his career in journalism hit a bump. He was still reeling from her cruelty, trying to understand how love could hurt so badly, and thus needed shelter while he learned his way through such difficult terrain. Kelly provided that, seeing to his material needs and helping to insulate him from most of society's expectations and demands. Tailing people was so far outside the norm that it hardly seemed real, which was exactly where Jarkey needed to be. Despite his snide critique of Kelly's behavior, he understood what the detective was doing for him and was grateful.

Munching his sandwich, he read the papers carefully, with some bitterness, analyzing the work of former colleagues until it was too dark to read. Then he turned on the radio and caught the beginning of a Jean Shepherd monologue about a pest exterminator who ran a have-a-heart trapping service up in Westchester. Shepherd's wry, friendly voice filled the night and salved Jarkey's wounds. This exterminator would trap the woodchucks off those big lawns and haul them away. Naive clients assumed he'd release the animals in the wilds upstate. The rest just figured he'd gas them or shoot them. But he didn't do any of that.

What he did was take them across town and release them on the lawns of the estates over there. Pretty soon he'd get calls from those people, and he'd go over and trap the woodchucks in his have-a-heart traps and let them go where he'd first caught them. He'd been at it for years: Spring and fall were the big seasons, and it was working out fine. The woodchucks were like his partners in the business. Whole generations of them. They'd waddle into the cages and wait patiently to be transported to their alternate digs. But then a competitor from Ardsley started releasing woodchucks on his turf. He could tell because the woodchucks were new and scared, hissing and clawing in the traps. "That," said Shep, "was when the trouble started."

Jarkey never got to hear the rest, because at that moment Kevin Gallagher came stomping out onto the sidewalk, slamming the building door. "Fucking bitch!" he yelled, then pounded off, hands jammed in his pockets.

This presented Jarkey with a tough call. Kelly'd told him to tail Gloria. But Gallagher now was there in front of him. And, clearly, the deeper purpose of his assignment—if such an escapade could be dignified with that term—was to get some dirt on Gallagher. Jarkey, watching him head down the block, slid out of the car, pushing the door quietly shut.

It turned out the right thing to do. Gallagher boarded the subway southbound. Jarkey sat a car back, keeping his eye on the platform at each stop. He exited behind Gallagher at Chambers Street and tailed him two blocks east to a stolid granite-fronted building. Though it was long after office hours for any regular sort of business, Gallagher pushed through the high brass doors with the unhesitating confidence of a man who knew exactly where he was going. Jarkey waited a couple of minutes, then walked past the entrance, glancing inside. The lobby was empty. He pushed through the brass doors and walked over to the directory on the wall next to the elevator.

They were all federal offices.

Agnes Day

Harry Jarkey, given his wounded condition, never considered how much he brought to the arrangement with Kelly. But the fact was, Kelly approved of him as a person, respected his work, and needed his assistance in such matters as finding car keys and tailing clients' daughters. Kelly had a profound understanding of his own existential helplessness. It was part of his power.

He stood examining the piles of photostats now spread out on his desk—all Jarkey's doing—full of admiration at what a genius his man was in a newspaper morgue. Jarkey understood the branching nature of reality, that stories were webs, not lines. What he'd given Kelly was more than a stack of reports about a dead woman, Agnes Mundi. It was the story of her world and how it intersected with her husband's. Somewhere in the overlap was the key to Richard. Kelly was sure of it. Once he understood those two, he could make sense of this mess with the daughter.

The lead on the obit, in bold type, said, "Agnes Day Mundi, 46, Entertainer." She'd been discovered dead in her home and, judging by the conflicting euphemisms, it was probably suicide. "Unexpected" might have been a heart attack, unlikely for a forty-six-year-old.

"Brave struggle" suggested a lingering illness, which didn't jibe with "unexpected"—unless it *had* been a lingering mental illness.

A few sheets down there was another story from two days earlier, entitled, "Singer Found Dead." It differed in an interesting, not to say heart-stopping, way from the obituary. This version suggested an autopsy was planned, which in turn suggested an overdose of narcotics as the cause of death. That put a different spin on "brave struggle." To Kelly it looked like the earlier item broke before anyone had a chance to whitewash it. By the time the obit came out, the story had been changed to imply suicide. Better that than a dying junkie.

Her stage name was Agnes Day but her family name was Dyckman, old money from upstate, relatives of the even older Manhattan Dyckmans. Jarkey had retrieved a pile of stuff about them. Railroads, canals, coal, a brewery. Properties they'd owned in Kingston before that place became a slum. Agnes had been a debutante during the Depression, which meant her family had deep-enough money to survive the thirties. She'd attended Bryn Mawr and had been married briefly to a man named Day who'd been killed in an auto-racing accident in 1938. Then she married Mundi, who was featured in the financial section later, in '47, as one of the "new breed" of developers "working closely with state and federal agencies to create high-quality affordable housing for returning servicemen." Mundi's file showed him creeping across Long Island, then into Manhattan and northern Jersey. No mention of Gloria, oddly, other than that she'd been born in '41. Prominent people didn't talk as much about their babies after Lindbergh.

Nor did women who were developing careers. And Agnes was definitely working on hers. There were a couple of pictures. She was pleasant enough to look at but must have lacked a leading lady's pizzazz. Probably it was Mundi's pull that got her to Broadway. Or maybe family connections. She'd worked in a number of supporting roles, character stuff mostly—the homely girlfriend or the eccentric aunt. The seeming pinnacle had come when she landed a gig as Vivian Blaine's understudy in *Guys and Dolls*. It should have been the start of bigger things, but it wasn't. She disappeared from the news for a couple of years, and when she showed up again it was, as Kelly dimly remembered her now, singing with the Harry James Orchestra. Then came a short review of a Village gig as a torch singer, then a blank until the death notice and obit in '60, which made it seven years she'd been dead rather than the ten Mundi had said. He'd been rounding off.

Somehow it had gotten to be late afternoon and Kelly still hadn't had breakfast. He thought of the jar of Tang, but instead took three aspirin and washed them down with a swig of Wilson's. Then he picked up the phone and after several tries connected with Nordbloom & Macomber, the agency that'd handled Agnes Day.

He spoke to a Mr. Lundquist, told him he was working on a feature article for the *Sunday Times* on the city's female vocalists, and there might be some ink for the sleeper acts that were every agent's burden. They made an appointment for an interview that would never come off, and while they were shooting the breeze Lundquist happened to mention Agnes. Kelly expressed interest in her and Lundquist told him the names of some of the places she'd worked in Manhattan before she died.

Kelly hung up satisfied, had another hit of Wilson's, took the train down to Bleecker Street, and walked west to the Swingin' Door. He knew the club and he knew the manager. It was here,

Lundquist had told him, in a rather dramatic fashion, that the curtain had come down for Agnes.

Smart money had set the place up Left Bank–style during the beatnik era. They billed name entertainment between the poetry sessions and packed the joint with tourists who wandered out of Washington Square thinking to experience the real thing at $1.50 a drink. But trade had fallen off, once fashion sent the decent folk uptown to twist. The Door started to swing shut, getting wilder and less profitable. The smart money sold out and left their partner, Kelly's pal Johnny Carburetor, holding the bag. Now the club was selling cheap shots to bums and waiting for hippies to start spending like advertising executives.

The alcove up front where the coat check girl used to stand was dark and smelled faintly of urine. Kelly winked at her ghost and went undisturbed down the four steps to the club itself. After all these years, he thought, the decor was finally looking authentic.

It was still early for a place like this. A few couples lurked in the shadows, and two alkies were sitting at a table down front. One of them kept drooping forward, then lurching up again. The other stared at his knee, letting his cigarette burn toward his first two fingers. Up on the stage a yellowed pianist was capably churning out cocktail tunes, wondering if it was time for his next fix.

The bartender sported black horn-rims and a close-trimmed goatee, and would've been the archetypal hipster except that he had a rummy's purple nose. He was sipping daintily from a filthy glass and reading a well-thumbed paperback. When Kelly sat down he slapped the book shut and grinned in recognition.

"Kelly! You ain't dead yet?" The gap between his two bottom teeth was just wide enough to accommodate his top tooth.

"Been too busy. Boss around?"

"Gone to read and write." Sandy was an old-timer.

"Took the air, eh?"

"Tap city," Sandy replied.

"They send him up the river or pull the plug?" Kelly was quickly losing track of what they were talking about.

"Johnny ain't dead, if that's what you mean. And he ain't in jail. Yet. Rounded up his assets and boogied. Musta hit a bad week at the track. Me and the musician get the stock and the nightly gate for keeping the place open. We're even taking liquor deliveries. Make the creditors think Johnny Boy's still in town. Haw haw."

The laugh turned into a coughing fit. Sandy poured the contents of the glass down his throat and the cough became a gurgle, then a purr.

"You've really turned the place around."

Sandy tilted his head in the direction of the piano. "Manny's got his habit to think about, and I might be at the end of my run here. Got a cousin in Vegas who'll put me up. Lotsa work out there."

Kelly went around behind the bar, made himself a drink, returned to his stool, and put down a $10 bill.

"The root of all evil," said Sandy, eyeing the money.

"You're an evil guy."

"So what's on your mind?"

"Agnes Day."

Sandy rubbed the mass of purple tissue that served as his nose and stared heavenward, as if his speech were printed on the stamped metal ceiling. "Agnes Day . . . Sure, I remember. A little dish of a redhead used to sing for Funko Williams's band."

"That was Alice Blake, Sandy. You got them confused."

"Oh yeah? Maybe I do." He folded the sawbuck twice and tapped the wad against his top tooth. Then he handed the bill to Kelly. "Tell you what. It took some trouble to get them confused. You'd save yourself a lot more if you did the same."

Kelly knew he was on to something now. He took another $10 bill, folded it with the first one, and slipped them under the book on the bar. Sandy was reading *Barnyard Lust*, a classic in its field. "Too late for staying out of trouble."

"Okay. Your funeral."

"And your twenty dollars. So tell me about Agnes. Who made you forget her?"

"Heavies. Scary guys like in the movies. They came around and gave Johnny and me the idea that it might be good to forget she was ever alive."

"Who sent them?"

"Mundi. That's my guess. He was sick in love with her, you know. I don't think he wanted word spread around about how bad she'd gotten."

"Couldn't hold a tune anymore?"

"Couldn't hardly stand up anymore. There was something really wrong with her. Probably strung out on downers. It was sad. He'd be sitting back there and you could see it was driving him crazy."

"When was this?"

"Fifty-nine. Not too long before she died."

"What was her act like by then?"

"She could never cut it as an actress, you know? But she had some pipes. Went with the big bands for a while, then I think the travel got to her. Started booking just local gigs with house bands. By the time she got here she was working with a tenor man, sorta like a white Billie Holiday. Had some talent, all right, but she was already a goner. Kept missing shows."

"How was she getting on with Mundi?"

"Oh, just great. He was a control freak and she was a prima donna. You can imagine what it was like at home. If she ever went home."

"So he wanted it hushed up to save her reputation?"

"Or his. That's what some people think, anyway."

"What do you think?"

Sandy looked around the room, then down at his book. Kelly peeled off another $10 bill. Sandy pocketed the three bills and looked hard at Kelly. "Where do you think his head was at, having this bitch tear his guts out every night? How hard you think it would have been for him to do something about it?"

"I thought you said he loved her."

"He loved what she was, not what she turned into. I know for a fact he had her in the hospital a couple of times. But it never took. If you want to know what I think, I think she was all twisted up inside, and it was just a matter of time before she killed herself in some lushed-out way. Right in front of all his rich friends. And I think that's why he wanted us to dummy up about her. The whole thing's a bummer. Leave it alone."

"Are you trying to tell me he let her kill herself?"

"I got no more to tell."

"Was it drugs or booze?"

"I'm sick of talking about it. I had to watch her ruin herself and her old man, too. I'm sorry you made me think about it."

"You realize how much her family was worth?"

"I told you I was finished, Kelly. Go away."

Nanny

They were supposed to meet at ten for coffee at the Copper Kettle, a little place around the corner from the Tishman Building, but Gloria didn't arrive until ten fifteen. Roth was waiting in a booth near the door, doodling with his mechanical pencil on the paper place mat. He winked at her when she came in, did not rise.

Julius Roth was somewhere between an uncle and a father to her. What with Mommy's struggle to manage her illness and her career, and Daddy's preoccupation with business, he'd done much of the actual work of raising her—driving her around, cooking for the three of them at the Westchester house when the staff was off, serving as her part-time nanny, bodyguard, and confidante. When she would run off to get into trouble, he'd anticipate her move and appear in front of her, arms folded over his huge chest, that indulgent ever-loving smile on his puss. It still felt that way. From the first, he'd been one of the few people she couldn't bully or charm into submission.

She didn't want any part of this meeting because she knew he was going to talk to her about Kevin, whom she didn't want to talk about because, although she'd seen through his egotism and phony romanticism, she was still getting her mind around the nearly unbearable fact that he'd used her. She wasn't ready to talk about it yet, at least not to Julie.

He eyed her as she slid into the booth, and she beamed at him—innocent as a dewy morning. "We've been missing you around the office, Glo."

"I've been trying to avoid everyone."

"Tired of my lectures?"

This had to be about Kevin. Or did it? "As tired as ever. But it's Daddy, really. Every time I see him these days, he tears into me."

"You know he loves you."

"He's got a funny way of showing it."

"He's been under a lot of pressure."

"Me, too."

Roth had always paid close attention to her and, thanks to enough carefully gathered intelligence, he had a pretty good idea of what was going on. In the course of her disillusionment with Gallagher and the *foco,* she'd become Irene Kornecki's full-time legal aide, using her smarts and manipulative ability to gather facts bearing on the most difficult cases. Now she was beginning to understand that Irene was vastly more effective than Gallagher's empty talk or any of the violent schemes of the Motherfuckers. More important, though he had no idea of the specifics of the matter, Roth sensed that Irene had become a certain kind of figure in her life—how could he put it?—a person she enjoyed beyond any question of use or gain. He knew this was a precious sort of relationship, one Gloria had rarely experienced.

He reckoned that her feelings for Irene had gotten mixed up with her anger at Gallagher, and the resulting emotional mess had spilled onto her father, whose self-absorption and dictatorial ways always made him an easy target. It didn't help that, in his burned-out state, he'd abdicated his parental duties along with just about everything else. The Newark windfall presented a perfect way to act out against her father while winning Irene's approval. Roth could sense she was determined to get her hands on it before Mundi could turn it to his own purposes.

She looked at her old friend gazing into his coffee cup and braced herself for the Kevin lecture.

But he surprised her. Roth told her about the heroin straight up—where it was, how it had been acquired, and how much it was worth. Then he laid down a lot of backstory she'd never heard before about Weehawken Mills, the utter uselessness of Murchison and Kraft, her father's increasing dysfunctionality, and the tremendous hit they'd taken after the Newark riots. Daddy had always wanted her to run the company. Now Roth was telling her that it was probably too late. There was nothing left to take charge of except a shell corporation and a lot of debt.

The only sane thing to do was to offer the "assets" of Mundi Enterprises to the bad guys in Newark, who would use them to legitimize the enormous amounts of cash their business generated. The return of the heroin would be the conversation starter, the peace offering.

"I want to take the initiative," Roth told her. "Get to them with the whole idea before they bang our doors down."

"What does this have to do with me?"

"I know you've been talking to Seamster. I know how much time you've been spending with your lawyer friend. I know you want that stuff and I'm pretty sure I know why you want it. And I have to tell you, I can almost agree with you. It would be a wonderful thing to put that filthy shit to some good use in this world."

Gloria gaped at him.

"But there are complicating factors," he added.

"Aren't there always?"

"Not like this. In the first place, your father doesn't intend to listen to me and give the drugs back to the Newark boys. He wants to sell them himself. Take the money and run."

"Are you sure?"

"Sugar, I've been around him so long, I can read his mind."

"So he's going to run off with the dope and leave you to deal with a pack of pissed-off mobsters?"

"That's not necessarily a huge problem. The really bad part is that he'll never get away with it. He thinks he's still in his prime, but he's too old, too slow. They'll find him and kill him. He doesn't stand a chance."

The waitress rattled past with a tray of empties. Roth asked for the bill.

"There's more, Glo, and this is the hard part." He turned to her earnestly. "I can't work for him anymore. Not with where his head is at."

"What would you do if you weren't working for Daddy?"

"I don't know. You, your father, the family . . . you've been my life for a long time. All I know is that right now I need to keep him from getting himself killed. Then I'll figure the rest out. That's why I'm asking you not to do anything that'll . . . complicate the situation. I mean with the heroin. You've got to give me some room here."

She grasped what he'd done and seethed. By coming clean with her, he was putting a moral roadblock in her way. A little more sophisticated, but not that much different than when she was little. "I didn't know any of this."

"It's okay, Glo. It'll work out fine. I just need your help."

"Of course, of course."

They were silent for a while, like chess players over the board. He was relieved she was listening, that she hadn't copped an attitude. She, despite her frustration at being headed off once again, was pleased he'd cut her some slack about Gallagher, that he seemed to understand about Irene and the cause. Each felt they were in the presence of a worthy adversary, and satisfied to have moved the game this far. The old Turk's load had them both.

She rose and gave him a peck on the forehead. She really did love him. She just wished he'd get the hell out of her way. Roth blushed with shy pleasure, like one of Snow White's dwarves. He adored her, knew she was almost ready to come into her own. She was so damned good at seeing people, at intuiting their weaknesses and needs. She was just a little too into herself, hadn't been knocked around by the world enough. That would come, if only he could convince her to play along this one last time.

He watched her through the window, smiling, as she headed toward the subway. Harry Jarkey watched her, too, from across the street. He folded his paper and followed her down.

Gloucester Harbor, Evening

All it took to be reborn into a new world was for the Mailman to realize he was as good as dead in the old. Then he was free to take advantage of the opportunity that had been in front of him all along but that he hadn't been able to see until his rebirth.

The new grand scheme had two parts.

The first was in the basement of the Historical Society. At the end of a long worktable were two paintings he'd wrapped and boxed. They were supposed to have been picked up on Thursday, but the restoration people had had to cancel and, because the museum was closed on Mondays, they would not return until Tuesday. So there they sat—*Gloucester Harbor, Evening* and *Brace's Rock*—two oils by Fitz Hugh Lane.

The Mailman knew all about Lane because the Society had a whole room devoted to him: a nineteenth-century American luminist painter who'd lived and worked in Gloucester. A recent article in the local paper had called him "America's first native marine painter of any importance." In the early twentieth century his work began coming out of local attics. Now his paintings were bringing up to six figures at fancy New York auctions.

For years *Gloucester Harbor* had hung over the main desk at the public library across the street. Then someone realized its potential value. The library trustees had a high-quality reproduction installed in the old frame and sent the original over to the Historical Society for safekeeping. A pinched old aristocrat who'd been one of the founders of the Society had earlier donated *Brace's Rock*, a little jewel of a luminist masterpiece. Now the two pictures were keeping each other company.

Recently a state grant had been approved to have both cleaned and reframed. That meant they were out of their frames, which made it perfect. Even with a layer of foam they'd fit neatly into a suitcase. In the normal course of things, paintings not on exhibition were stored in the vault, but that wouldn't have mattered. The director himself had lost the keys to the vault years before, and now it was always unlocked.

The second part of the scheme was down in New York, a guy he'd known early on in his postal career, who'd lived for a while on the top floor of his apartment house on Portugee Hill. He was the black sheep of a family made wealthy by a string of auto dealerships. He'd started off in drugs, but seemed to prefer art and antiques, which were in no short supply in Massachusetts in the fifties and early sixties. He'd learned the trade under a smooth old swamp Yankee, and boasted that he and his mentor had been in every house on Cape Ann, omitting the fact that half of those entries had been uninvited. After burning through the North Shore he'd headed for New York. Supposedly he'd gotten back into drugs, but the chances were good that he'd still know what to do with a few hundred thousand dollars' worth of art.

The Mailman went back upstairs and left a note informing the staff that he had an afternoon doctor's appointment. He walked past generous three-story white and yellow wooden frame houses, and down the hill to the tumble of old brick and stone bars, brothels, marine supply stores, and sail lofts that lined Water Street, to the offices of CIA.

Continental Insurance Agency was a waterfront joke. The acronym was, anyway, since the putative insurance agency was a cover for illegal activities ranging from short lobsters to bales of marijuana, shipments of cocaine or heroin, and weaponry for the IRA. Nothing else about them, however, was risible. CIA had once been on the Mailman's route and, though he hadn't been in the building for years, his familiarity with the layout gave him a sufficient comfort level that he could dispense friendly nods to the roomful of thick-browed Sicilians smoking and playing pinochle, and walk unchallenged up the stairs to the air-conditioned office where the occasional COD or Adult Signature Required had been delivered.

Mr. Reardon rose from behind his desk, only half surprised to see the Mailman. The slouched form was instantly recognizable, even if the face was now obscured by a dark beard. He thought, reflexively, that there might be a package for him, then remembered what he'd heard of the Mailman's story—the cancer, the drugs. Poor miserable junkie. The guy was here to tap him.

"Merster Eardon."

The sounds the Mailman made grated in his ears.

"Come on in. Siddown." He'd give him $50—once—Reardon decided, and that would be the end for him at CIA. The thought of junkies felt like lice in his clothes.

That feeling shot past the Mailman, stoned on his scheme, as high as he'd ever been. It was better than smack, better than being in love. If he was going to be dead anyway, he might as well do this thing.

"I nee to fie Lloy Samberlan."

Reardon, who'd been preparing to dispense a handout and some tough love, was confused, could not parse the burp-talk.

The Mailman pulled out his pad, printed, *I need to find Lloyd Chamberlain,* and pushed it across the desk.

Reardon nodded, relieved. Chamberlain was one of the rats the lice lived on. The Mailman wanted in on some kind of low-level drug deal. Well, that would be easy enough, and save him $50 to boot. He consulted his books, wrote a phone number and an address on the pad, and handed it back, eyeing the Mailman coldly.

"Don't come back here," Reardon said.

"Doan worry," the Mailman burped.

Standing in the Shadows

After three days of standing in the shadows, of being one with the Fairlane, of extended bladder management, of disciplined, grinding surveillance, Jarkey was getting a good sense of her routine. That gave him a better opportunity to pick his spots so he could be sure the lighting was right—always a critical factor when using a telephoto lens. Kelly wanted lots of photos. He said pictures always made his clients feel they were getting their money's worth.

Jarkey snapped away—Gloria leaving her pad in the Village, Gloria in the Lower East Side at Gallagher's place. Gloria up at Morningside Heights heading to an office in the front of a first-floor apartment, to visit a looker whose name turned out to be Irene Kornecki. Those visits happened in the afternoon. She'd leave Gallagher's with a briefcase or an armful of folders, spend a few hours up on 116th, then go home to Bank Street empty-handed. Jarkey used the backward directory to get the phone number for the address, called it, and heard a woman's voice say, "Irene Kornecki's office."

Jarkey suspected she might be an MD in on a drug ring being run by Gallagher as a sting for the Feds. He told the voice that he'd like an appointment. The lady asked him for a brief description of the problem. He told the lady he had a pain in his lower back and was informed that he'd reached a legal office, not a doctor. That changed his suspicion about the drug ring.

A little asking around got him the information that Kornecki was a Columbia Law grad on a short list of lawyers to whom civil rights demonstrators were referred. That meant dozens of minor beefs, hence the folders. When, on the afternoon of the fourth day, Kornecki got out of a cab in front of Gallagher's, the loop was closed.

In all, it'd been an excellent run.

Jarkey picked up the last of the photos from the lab, put them in with his notes, then went over to Fifty-Third, collected Kelly, and drove him uptown and down, to Kornecki's, Gallagher's, and Gloria's, taking him through their various movements. Particulars were important to the detective.

Once he was sure Kelly had all the locations down pat, he laid out the narrative that accompanied the images. Gloria and her boyfriend were working for the Feds, dishing them info about demonstrators and other revolutionary types under the cover of doing legal work for the movement with this Kornecki person.

Kelly nodded slowly, in a way that mimicked deep thought. Of course there was no thinking going on, but Jarkey understood that Kelly's act was a demonstration of respect for all his hard work. "I like it, Jark. Not what I expected, but I like it. It hangs together, doesn't it?"

"Given the facts, I don't see a more plausible story."

"It's gonna blow the old man's mind, that's for sure. If I tell him."

"Kelly, for crissakes, you're getting *paid* to tell him."

"I'm not getting paid to blow the cover of a couple of federal agents."

"Well, it's your call." By this time Jarkey was double-parked in front of Sammy's.

"Join me for dinner?"

"I don't think so. I've got some other stuff to wrap up."

Though he was fond of Norbert, the scene at Sammy's was too lushed out for his tastes, and he knew that Kelly's "dinner" would involve a dozen whiskeys. He drove back to Bank Street, parked the car in its usual spot, then walked over to a Greek diner on Hudson for a burger and more coffee.

He was feeling good about the job and about himself. One more day of surveillance, just to put the lid on it, then the case would be done. Once Gloria's old man found out what she was up to, he'd back off. It was such a neat package that Kelly might even find himself in a bonus situation. They'd get paid and nobody would get hurt.

It started to rain while Jarkey ate. Umbrellas came out. He put his *Daily News* over his head and walked fast back to Kelly's car. As he approached it he saw someone leaning against the front fender. A woman. Hooker, but maybe not. He didn't see anyone suspicious among the random passersby, but that didn't make him any less concerned. He thought about going back for another coffee, waiting until she moved along. Then he realized, to his horror, that she was making eye contact. He drifted to the far edge of the sidewalk, hiding under his newspaper.

"Hey! Don't forget your car."

His head jerked around involuntarily and he looked at the woman. It was Gloria. She'd made him. His shoulders slumped. He stopped and squinted at her through his glasses.

"You talking to me?" He'd fucked it up. The whole deal was ruined now. She'd run to her father and a week of work would go down the drain.

She pushed herself off the fender and faced him, calm and erect, tan raincoat cinched tight around the waist, hair tied back, red scarf. "Aren't you the gentleman who's been following us around this week?"

The way she phrased it made him feel foolish. Who followed people around, anyway? Losers like Kelly, that was who. "Lady, I'm just a working man."

It was worse now that he could see her face. Composed, unafraid. "Sitting in that car all day? I mean, really . . ." Moving toward him. "Don't worry. I didn't tell."

She was making fun of him. He glared at her, shamed and indignant. "Tell who?"

She cocked her head. "Give me a break."

She was actually quite pretty. Very relaxed, a hint of mirth about her, as if the whole thing were some kind of joke. He realized belatedly that Gallagher and his pals could materialize at any moment and make a mess of him. But that did not happen. This was more than a confrontation. Something else was going on. He took a chance at an explanation and blurted, "I'm just the guy that got hired by the guy . . ."

It wasn't coming out right but she got it. She chuckled, surprisingly deep, up from the chest. "Give me a minute with that one."

He was smiling now, despite himself. She was head-tripping him. But it felt better than being beaten up. "What do you want?"

"A little information, that's all."

"I'm having trouble with the 'that's all' part."

"Fair enough." She turned to the passenger door and motioned him to the driver's side. "Let's get out of the rain. Then you can tell me whom you're working for for." Making fun of his deer-in-the-headlights admission.

He got in the car and thought for a second about just driving off, leaving Gloria at the curb. But what would that get him? He reached across the seat and unlocked her door. Gloria slid in and turned toward him, giving him a glimpse of trim ankles, tight black leotard curving up under the coat.

"If you don't, I'll rat you out. I'll tell my father about you sitting in your big black car, and you'll look like a dope."

"Well, he was the one who hired us, so I don't know how far you'll get with that."

It came out meaner than he'd intended, but she didn't flinch. "My father, huh?"

"He said he was worried about you."

"That's rich. There's only one person he worries about these days, and it's not me. Anyway, how much fun do you think it is, feeling like someone's watching you all the time?"

How long had she been on to him? Jarkey turned and blinked at her. A smile began in her eyes and moved to her mouth—mischievous, conspiratorial.

Jarkey wasn't having any. "I know what the deal is, Gloria."

"What's the deal?"

"About what you and Gallagher are doing to those poor dopes who think they're going to start a revolution."

"What are you talking about?"

"Come off it. The photos are sitting in Kelly's office right now. The negatives are somewhere else."

"Photos of what?"

"Photos of your boyfriend walking out of the downtown field office of the FBI. Photos of you talking to him an hour later."

Her face went blank, then white. At that moment he saw that her features were quite delicate—exquisite, actually, in a way that belied her glib toughness. Then they bunched themselves into the deepest scowl. She said, "Shit," once, softly, and turned from him, toward the passenger door.

That was when Jarkey fell for her.

An American Place

Kelly spent a few hours in his office assembling the information he'd gathered, which consisted of the photographs Jarkey had taken, each one with the date and time printed in a white rectangle at the bottom, to correspond with his field notes. The man was brilliant.

As he sifted through them Kelly thought back on what he'd seen of Gloria at Lloyd's party. It was hard to imagine a rich girl like her working as a stoolie for the FBI. Harder still to imagine *why* she'd do such a thing. Whatever the reasons, it was a risky place for her to be. Her father would not be happy to hear about it.

But he was going to hear it anyway, and soon. Kelly dialed Mundi's office and made an appointment for late afternoon. Then he took a long, hot shower.

Kelly's office, with its efficiency unit adjoining, was in a venerable building on the corner of Fifty-Third and Madison. The place had formerly been occupied by a shady business type who, after a wrangle with the IRS, was forced by bankruptcy to vacate. Mr. Hurst, the landlord, then cut Kelly a deal on the remainder of the lease. The truth was, Hurst owed him. He'd hired the detective when he'd begun to suspect his soon-to-be third wife of serious gold-digging.

Kelly (Jarkey, actually) had uncovered a forgotten husband to whom, it seemed, she was still married. Hence the break on the office.

As he buttoned his shirt, Kelly thought about Mr. Hurst and his encyclopedic knowledge of Manhattan real estate, how he must've known Richard Mundi back in the old days. He might even have something to add to Sandy's sad narrative and the stark facts contained in the clippings Jarkey had gathered. He picked up the phone.

Fortunately Mr. Hurst was just about to step out for his daily constitutional when Kelly called. They met on the corner of Fifth and Seventy-Sixth, and hiked together up to the Met where, with no one but yawning guards to overhear them, they discussed Richard Mundi.

Mundi, Hurst recalled, had married Agnes Day at the beginning of his career. There'd been a society wedding, quite a do. She'd had some kind of show business connection, and the papers made a fuss about it all. But he'd never seen her perform. Then some scandal, but, unfortunately, Hurst wasn't exactly certain what it involved. She died young, he knew that much. Mundi himself had been a comer when he'd first arrived on the scene, brash but appealing. A solid man to drive a deal with. Of the daughter, Gloria, he knew nothing.

They were back on the street by this time, and the older man watched with something approaching awe as Kelly inhaled a hot dog, a Yoo-hoo, and two non-filter Kools. Then they shook hands and parted company, Hurst to a meeting with his accountant, and Kelly—though his friend had told him nothing he didn't already know—deeper into the misguided certainty that Agnes Day Mundi's untoward death was the key to the entire case.

The Voice on the Other End

The phone was ringing, ringing. More to stop it than anything else, Chamberlain grabbed it, held it to his ear. The voice on the line was ghastly, doomed. At the raw end of a binge, Lloyd didn't feel much better himself.

"Lloy. Lloy, is dat eeeh-yeww?"

"Who is this?"

"Lloy. Z'mee. D Mayomann. Member mee?"

"Jesus God." Survival instinct took over. Lloyd humored the voice, cajoled it, terrified. He knew who it was. Hung up.

Took barbiturates, tried to sleep, got sick, knowing he'd dreamed it, knowing he hadn't. Tried to masturbate, couldn't. Drank fluids, suddenly ravenous, thirsty. Drank more, ate, felt sick, got sick, slept for a few seconds.

Woke to an electric jolt of terror. Picked up the phone and dialed.

"Kelly, it's Lloyd."

"Lloyd. What's going on?"

"He called me, Kelly. *He* fucking called me up an hour ago. He told me who he was, and I knew it was *him*. I mean I knew he was this guy I used to know back in Massachusetts. But it wasn't."

"What the hell are you talking about?"

"It was *him,* Kelly."

"Who, Lloyd?"

"The guy I told you about last week. The guy they fucking put the *brain* into."

"Oh, him."

"He got my phone number, Kelly. *Nobody* has my phone number, you dig? He must have gotten it from the computers." Lloyd could hear Kelly thinking. He knew what those thoughts must be. He didn't care, though. He was too scared. "I need your help, man. *He* says *he's* coming here."

"When?"

"Tonight. Just a few hours. Says *he's* got something he fucking wants to *show* me."

"Well, maybe he does."

"Kelly, I need a place to stay for a while. Can you help me?"

"You got any downers over there?"

"Of course."

"Take them. And a bunch of vitamins and hot soup. Hot soup is good. I've got one appointment uptown, then I'll be over. I'll talk to him for you. You won't even have to be in the room. He probably won't show up anyway."

Kelly wasn't thinking about the guy with the brain. He was thinking about Helen, imagining her being there with Chamberlain. Maybe he'd send Lloyd over to his place after all, then wait around with Helen to see what happened next.

Face Man

Gloria and Jarkey were still sitting in Kelly's car outside her apartment. The rain had not let up. It was the warm, tropical kind, so they had to keep the windows cracked to prevent the car from fogging. Gloria took off the scarf and shook her hair out. She'd regained her composure and dropped the flirty stuff. Jarkey explained to her who and what Kelly was, how he'd come to Richard Mundi's attention, and what Mundi had hired him to do. That, while Kelly was off investigating other aspects of the case, he'd been given the job of tailing her. His only other option to this lengthy explanation would have been silence, and Jarkey now did not want silence with this woman.

"I found out about Gallagher and the Feds that first night. It was just luck. And he was sloppy."

"He's always been sloppy."

"So I had what I needed on him, but I thought I'd better make sure about you. I assumed you were in on the deal. When I found out you were working with Kornecki, it all seemed to fit together. I guess I was sloppy myself."

"No, you were fine. It was the car, actually. I've got a thing about cars. Yours has a ding on the front fender. I knew I'd seen it down by Kevin's place, and I thought I remembered it being parked on this street before. I was just standing there trying to figure out what to do and you walked along."

"How did you know to yell at me?"

"You had this incredible look . . ."

It had been more than half an hour and Jarkey was still enthralled. "Kind of you to put it that way."

"Meanwhile I've been letting that asshole spy on us for the Feds. Talk about sloppy. And that's not the worst of it."

"There's more?" He was surprised to realize that she seemed on the verge of trusting him, which only enhanced the attraction of her lovely, quirky eyes. Jarkey was quirky himself in that respect: While most American males had breast or leg fixations, he was a face man. Gloria had the kind of face that did things to him.

For her part, Gloria was equally surprised at the turns this meeting was taking. Discovering that she was being followed pissed her off. She'd intended initially to hassle Jarkey, verify her suspicion that Daddy had sent him, then humiliate him. But taking in his earnest, toothy face behind those glasses, his nonconfrontational attitude, and his thinly disguised fascination with her, she realized she'd hit the jackpot with this guy. If she wanted, she could have him on all fours, barking like a dog.

But she didn't want that. In an inspired moment of improvisation she saw that some use might be made of him and that she ought to keep him around for a while, see what developed. So she gave him a conditional half-smile, as if deciding whether to come clean. She waited a beat, then let go.

"It's the craziest thing. Right in the middle of the Newark riots there was some kind of accident, and my father's people came into a load of heroin. From what I can figure, it was a delivery that went bad. The long and the short is that Daddy's holding now. In his safe at the office. It's worth a lot of money. A whole lot."

Jarkey, who'd been listening carefully, nodded. Pushed the glasses back on his nose. He understood without her saying any more. "Port of Newark. Has to be Mob stuff. They must be looking for it."

"Umm. Daddy knows. Or rather Julie Roth knows. His right-hand guy. He actually runs the company. But that's not the real problem."

"Oh?"

"The problem is that I told Kevin. I had this brilliant idea that we could get it from Daddy, fence the stuff off, and set up a legal aid fund. Sort of what Irene and I are doing, but on a far bigger scale. I didn't think about people coming after Daddy."

"Well, they'll be after him, all right. Right now they're probably squeezing everyone in Newark. Someone's bound to talk sooner or later."

"Actually, that was when it started getting truly weird with Kevin. I mean, after I told him, he got real squirrelly. Wanted me to shut up about it. Pretended he was waiting for exactly the right time to tell the rest of the *foco*. But it didn't take me long to see through that. He wanted it for himself. The big score."

"And now the FBI knows your father has it."

"God, I'm such a dope."

Jarkey took a chance and reached across the seat and touched her arm. "You're not a dope, Gloria. We can figure this out. There may be time. For one thing, Kelly's probably briefing your father right now. When he hears Gallagher's working for the Feds, he'll dump the drugs fast."

"But he's got no idea Kevin knows about the drugs. I doubt he even suspects I know."

"That's something you need to fix."

Gloria wore a suitably worried expression, but in her private assessment things were shaping up nicely. These two detectives would create a diversion, some kind of mess. Then the FBI would show up, get real busy with Daddy, and she'd be in California turning a deal with her Berkeley people before anyone was the wiser.

"Let's go inside a minute. I've got to get my head together. Then we'll go uptown and talk to Roth. Can you drive me?"

"Sure."

Now she touched his arm. "You will keep quiet about this, won't you?"

"Count on it." He was thrilled.

Shoot the Messenger

Mundi was irritable when Kelly showed up at his office. But as he rooted through the pile of 8 × 10 glossies, his breathing slowed.

No way hiring this gumshoe had been anything but a colossal mistake. Getting rid of Gallagher wasn't going to fix anything with Gloria. In fact, putting a snoop on her was likely to make it worse. He'd meant to call Kelly off the day after their interview, but he'd gotten so distracted by the problem in his safe that it slipped his mind.

Julie was right, of course, about what to do with the stuff. The best thing for Mundi Enterprises, and the safest thing for himself, would be to give it back to the Newark boys. But Richard Mundi was having a hard time caring about Mundi Enterprises anymore, especially if it was going to turn into a Mob money-laundering operation. Even Murchison could see that. If he made any kind of a stink about anything, they'd kill him. So why not just steal the heroin himself? If he fucked up, they'd kill him. But he was as good as dead anyway.

So after that frustrating meeting with Murchison and Kraft and, despite their disapproval, he'd authorized Roth to make inquiries of Mr. DiNoto. This bought him time to solidify a deal with an independent in Chicago who'd take the smack and all the risk it entailed, and pay him $50K. A joke, but still better than nothing.

And all this time Kelly had been out there snapping photos of Gloria like some fucking paparazzi after Jackie K. As he flipped through them, Mundi's irritation shifted to deep antipathy.

"What's this?"

"That's Gallagher leaving the offices of the FBI on Chambers Street. He and your daughter have infiltrated a cell of activists on the Lower East Side. Gallagher's just reported to his handlers."

"You saying my daughter's a rat?"

"No."

"What, then?"

"Most likely she's protecting Gallagher. Though she does have some involvement with Lloyd Chamberlain, a known drug dealer. I've seen her at his place. Maybe the Feds are holding that over her. Some kind of connection with this pusher Chamberlain."

"A drug rap?"

"I said 'maybe.'"

Mundi looked up at Kelly, bent over the desk beside him. Shiny gray shave, whiff of Skin Bracer and Ipana covering stale booze breath. A born fucking loser. Trying to tell him his daughter was a stoolie, strung out on drugs. This creep had his head up his ass.

"You know this other girl?"

Kelly nodded. "A member of the cell. She does their legal work."

In fact, Mundi recognized her. She was Irene Kornecki, one of Gloria's Columbia buddies. Smart as a whip. Gloria had brought her around once and she'd put the bite on him for a donation to some lefty legal aid fund.

Then, a photo of Gloria and Gallagher. "This one was taken just after Gallagher left the federal building. He's probably briefing her on the meeting. That opens another possibility."

Mundi looked at him, hard, as mere dislike escalated into loathing. Was it something chemical, psychological? Did Kelly's face, physique, or odor trip some old bad memory in Richard Mundi? Humans could explain it any number of ways. To the old Turk's load, from its exalted perspective over in Mundi's safe, the matter boiled down to simple physics. Kelly was spinning and Mundi was standing still. Their collision released strange energy. Though it felt like hatred to Mundi.

Kelly caught the vibe. He read it as intense guilt on Mundi's part. The man had to be hiding something. He decided to run the Agnes angle up the flagpole and see how Mundi reacted.

"The other possibility is that the Feds know about your wife. They could be holding it over Gloria's head somehow."

"My wife?"

"The manner of her death. The, umm, overdose? I've done some research. I've talked to Dennis Hurst."

"Who?" But Kelly saw him stiffen slightly.

Mundi didn't say anything more because, at that moment, he was incapable of speech. The room faded to a distant spec and the universe roared in his ears. He stared past Kelly with an intensity that propelled him beyond Gloria and Gallagher, to Gloria graduating from college, to the painful years the two of them spent together after Agnes's death, to that death and his own guilt, to Agnes and himself in the brief moments of their happiness, to his wedding, to the first time he saw Agnes, and down, down time's dark shaft. A man alone in an elevator whose cable had snapped.

Kelly looked at Mundi, pale and perspiring, and believed he'd somehow been the messenger of bad tidings regarding the late Agnes. The man probably thought her suicide, overdose, or murder —whichever nasty end she'd come to—had been successfully covered up. Now he was going to have to deal with the idea that the authorities were wise to him.

But Kelly didn't know the half of it.

At that moment, as the elevator plunged on, Mundi was seriously contemplating shooting the messenger—not because his tidings were bad, but because the messenger was such a colossal idiot, and because his message had so rudely poked a tender spot in Mundi's otherwise leathery psyche. He had a little .22 with a silencer in the second drawer, good only up to a few feet, but if he held it right against whatever this moron had for brains. . . . Then he took a calming breath and thought about Agnes in her best moments and how, as soon as he settled this business with the Mob, he'd do right by her and be the cause of Kelly's slow and painful death.

Then he'd go after Gallagher. No, Seamster could handle that one. Or even better, they'd set it up so that Kelly would walk in on it, and they'd hang Gallagher's murder on him.

Maybe Gloria would figure it out, maybe not. It hardly mattered. It was too late with her, anyway. It was too late with everything. Before he left he was going to take Gallagher out, and Kelly, too. This nitwit was going to help with his own execution, somehow. It'd just take a little planning.

"Okay, Kelly, here's what you do. Drop the surveillance on Gloria and set something up for Gallagher. Something messy. And this time keep me informed. Every day. I want to know what's going on. Understand?"

"Sure. It'll take me a few days. But it shouldn't be a problem. A brick of pot in his pad ought to do the trick. The cops'll have him busted before the Feds get wise, and that'll be the end of his cover. Meanwhile, do you need any help managing the situation with the FBI and your wife?"

Shoot the messenger. Absolutely.

Mr. Fungu

The Street Brothers and Mr. Fungu double-parked at the corner of Fifty-Second and rumbled through the lobby of the Tishman Building like a line squall crossing Long Island Sound. Woody was making a list of Jewish ballplayers while Vince was scrupulously avoiding thought. Mr. Fungu was a brain-dead sociopath who couldn't think at all, which was why his associates referred to him as *u fungu*—the Mushroom.

Julius Roth had indeed approached Mr. DiNoto in Newark via an intermediary, but the initiative had come far too late. Mr. D. did not respond. Instead he had told the Street Brothers that Richard Mundi was holding the smack that had gone missing in the Newark riots. Now they were taking the Mushroom over to Mundi's office to trash the joint and frighten—not kill—Mundi. Then they were to keep an eye on Mundi's operation—seeing who came and went. If—as Mr. D. was almost certain—Mundi was personally holding the goods, he'd try to move the stash somehow. Or maybe if they frightened him enough, he'd simply give it back. Then they could kill him.

As they rode the elevator to the thirtieth floor, Woody considered the mighty Hank Greenberg, who had movie-star looks and a couple of great home run seasons to his credit but who may have looked like a better player than he was, since he never, in the course of a rather short career, learned to catch the baseball. Al Rosen was another Hymie with a short career. But he'd proved himself a good defensive player with a sweet swing and a sterling character. Always seemed to come through in the clutch.

They found the door with the golden ME monogrammed on it and swarmed in, upsetting the coffee table piled with magazines and barging through to the main office where the receptionist sat. Seamster came out of his office, sized the situation up, and reached around back for his gun. Vince kicked him in the knee before he got to it, then frisked his crumpled form and confiscated the weapon. Woody swept the front desk of its contents, ripped the phones out, and kicked Seamster's knee again just to keep him occupied. The Mushroom stood by the door, a promise of worse to come. Of course, Woody thought, there was Larry Sherry, who'd shut down the Go-Go White Sox in the '59 World Series. Had one or two good years at the end of the fifties, then what? Must've been arm trouble.

The Brothers surveyed the damage they'd caused, then walked into Mundi's office unannounced and sat down. Vince had Seamster's gun in his lap.

Mundi surveyed them, grim and red-faced. "Who are you and what the fuck are you doing in my office?"

Woody did the talking. "This is a courtesy call on behalf of our employer, Mr. DiNoto of New Jersey. Maybe you've heard of him."

"Let's get something straight. You guys don't scare me. If DiNoto wants to talk to me, he can get his own ass over here."

"Mr. D. doesn't care if he scares you or not. He happens to know you're holding some property of his and he wants it back."

"Why don't you tell him I'd be happy to talk with him about that very thing."

Then the Mushroom entered the office, lumbered between the two chairs, and pushed the huge mahogany desk toward Mundi, steadily and effortlessly, like an earthmover, pinning him against the tall glass window with one arm under the front of the desk, where it had been trying to extract the silenced .22. Mundi thrust his free arm out in an involuntary effort to fend off the looming monster. The Mushroom cracked it at the wrist.

Woody waited until lack of breath forced Mundi to stop screaming. Then he said, "We'll give you a day to think about it." And the squall moved on. The greatest of them all, of course, was the incomparable Koufax, recently retired, totally dominant.

Agent Spaulding

While Mr. Fungu and the Street Brothers were doing their thing in the Tishman Building, another office drama was taking place downtown, where Agent Spaulding was reading Kevin Gallagher the riot act. It'd been more than a year and Gallagher hadn't turned up shit. Now Spaulding's superiors were getting ready to terminate the operation, unless Gallagher provided something dramatic enough to make them pay attention.

"You're really pushing it, Gallagher. That bomb idea of yours was a complete dud. I think you need to get that kid Leo and . . . are you listening?"

Gallagher tilted his head toward the ceiling and launched three perfectly formed smoke rings. Spaulding liked to think he was tough, but he had freckles and pink skin and was running to plumpness, with a spare tire already gathering itself around him. Gallagher detested fat. Took it as a sign of moral weakness. He also had issues with authority. He ached to bust Spaulding's nose into his face, just as he'd once done to his father. It had felt so good. You could almost see the SPLAT like in *Batman*. Of course there'd been no choice after that except to leave home, and some of the things that had happened subsequently were difficult. But he'd survived. The experience had toughened him and he'd learned about people, learned how important it was to make deals. Like the one he and Spaulding had going.

He'd been running with a bad crowd in Wilmington, and they'd busted him for grand theft auto—a cheesy, trumped-up rap worth eighteen months, which he could do standing on his head, except he'd already been in once and this would make him a two-time loser. The next time they popped him, they'd put him away till his teeth all fell out. So there he was, in the county lockup waiting for his useless court-appointed counsel, when Agent Spaulding showed up in his cheap suit and shiny black shoes with a deal.

It had sounded pretty good in the context of the New Castle County detention facility. Spaulding showed him a photograph and asked if he'd ever seen the guy before, and Gallagher tumbled right away to what the deal was. He was supposed to rat out this hippie-looking guy in the photo. Then maybe Spaulding would help him cop a plea. So he told Spaulding what he knew—that the guy had approached Gallagher in a bar. Laid all this political shit on him and persuaded him to attend an antiwar rally. No big thing. The hippie had been buying the drinks.

Then Spaulding told him he wouldn't have to bargain a plea because the beef was going to go away. Disappear. All charges dropped. The only thing Gallagher had to do was help Agent Spaulding gather some information about this guy and his friends and their activities. In return Gallagher would get immunity and witness protection if he needed it. He'd be helping his country and he'd be paid for his time. The money would go into an escrow account. This would be his chance to turn his life around, a life they both knew was headed nowhere. It was a no-brainer. For his part, Gallagher figured he'd string Spaulding along for a while, then give him the slip.

But Spaulding had an answer for that. In the course of working his way into the antiwar movement Gallagher amassed a series of trespassing and disturbing-the-peace charges. Then in New York, with the Motherfuckers and the radical SDS wing who wanted to "Bring the War Home," he landed a breaking-and-entering beef. Next there was an arrest in a Vietnam protest, which produced a *Times* photo of him in handcuffs, between two burly cops. Spaulding let him know that if he walked on the FBI now, he'd be a fugitive. A man with a record and half a dozen charges outstanding. The escrow account, already up to seven grand, would disappear.

Talk about short hairs. The part that made Gallagher perversely think of his dad was how this exercise of absolute power was so small-time. Maybe there really *were* bomb-throwing revolutionaries out there, but Spaulding could never have penetrated their ranks because they were too smart. Instead, he was going after idealistic college kids, hoping to goad them into some desperate action that the FBI could thwart at the last minute, all in service of proving that bomb-throwing radicals existed and thus putting Spaulding's people in line for more funding. It was a pathetic, sick joke, with Gallagher trapped in the middle of it.

Except that now, thanks to Gloria and her old man's lucky find, he had another card to play.

Bank Street

In her Bank Street apartment, Gloria and Harry were smoking a quick joint and listening to *Revolver*, which they agreed was more innovative than the long-awaited *Sergeant Pepper*. They intended to find Roth and let him know about Gallagher and the FBI.

"Do you think I could just tell him on the phone? I mean, we've got to call him anyway and find out if he's even there." She gave it her kittenish best. Let this guy think he was in the driver's seat.

Jarkey sat across from her, feeling the reefer hit, uncertain in that stoned way, willing enough to be in her company, and seriously happy to have his every muscle and nerve telling him that he was back in the game, a sexual being once again, rather than a wounded animal. Finally he'd emerged from the shadow of his miserable ex. He watched Gloria blow a strand of hair from her face with exhaled smoke and concentrated on keeping the situation in the moment, hardly daring to hope what might come next. He told her, "You definitely need to talk to him in person. There could be a lot of questions. Maybe you should try to get your father in on it, too."

"It's just so hard to talk to Daddy. I know he'll freak. Julie will explain it rationally."

"Yeah, I can see that. Roth'll keep it clean. Figure out what to do."

"Exactly. Then Daddy can blow his top at me."

"What's his problem, anyway? It's not like you joined a motorcycle gang."

"I might as well have. Daddy thought I'd get my law degree and run the company."

"Umm, Kelly told me about that. And ... ?"

"I always thought I would, too. I just changed, I guess."

"Changed?"

"Okay. Not changed. I turned out to be somebody neither of us was expecting."

"Who was that?"

Jarkey wasn't a handsome man. His looks might have been "interesting" in the best possible light. But he had one great ability with women. He knew how to listen. Gloria, starting slowly, spun it out for him—the early happy nuclear family, her mother's deterioration. The chaos that followed her death. Daddy's loss, and the strange sense of guilt he carried. The bond she'd formed with him in those early teenage years. Then, inexplicable to them both, her equally intense rejection of him. His increasing disapproval. His distance.

"So that's where it's at. I couldn't even tell you how I feel about him now. There's just so much history in the way."

Gloria never said the word *remorse,* but Harry thought he could hear that feeling in her voice, as if they were having a second, unspoken conversation. She really was quite beautiful.

The doorbell rang.

Jarkey, yanked from his erotic reverie, hit the ceiling, then slumped back on the couch, paradise in shards around him. Whoever this was, the shape of the evening would now change, along with the outcome he was so ardently trying not to hope for.

Kelly and the Night Visitor

Kelly had picked up Lloyd's paranoia. He could hear the visitor clumping up the stairs to the apartment and could not fight off visions of a Frankenstein creature—big scar, spikes and wires coming out of the head. His fingers trembled as he unbolted the door, and the visitor's black beard and drug-worn face did not set him at ease. The gargling noises that came out of the man's mouth made Kelly jump, despite himself.

He peered from inside the still-chained door, .38 at the ready, and shuddered as the other man leaned his head back and pointed to the long scar that ran up his throat and terminated in a black hole beneath his chin. Lloyd had been right! No, he hadn't. "Droat cancer," the guy rasped. "Droat cancer. Gan't dalk." Kelly undid the chain and let him in, pistol squarely on him, frisked him, found him clean except for a half-empty bottle of pills, pointed him and his shabby suitcase to the couch.

Beyond delivering the medical report, the visitor would not state his business, indicating he'd talk only to Lloyd. With that horrible non-voice, taciturnity was inevitable. The man seemed glum, tired, sunk down inside himself, but utterly resolute. Kelly didn't doubt he'd sit there till the cows came home, suitcase between his knees.

Then, to Kelly's surprise, Lloyd emerged from the bedroom. Apparently he was sufficiently rested, hydrated, or sedated that his neurons had resumed firing along their accustomed circuits. The vision of the brain-in-the-jar had faded, for the time being, to its alternate status as a tortured imagining. Lloyd gave the man a thorough, cautious look, nodded, and sat down across from him. He turned on the floor lamp beside his chair, which only seemed to enhance the murk that pervaded the room. The rain had stopped and now it was getting dark. Grayish brown light was leaking in the big front window.

"What the fuck are you doing here?"

The Mailman threw his head back, gestured, and burped his way through the throat cancer story one more time.

"How'd you find me?"

"Eardon. CIA."

"How's Schultzie?"

"Okay."

Kelly put his gun away.

As Lloyd grilled his visitor about Gloucester and old times, the interrogation became a reminiscence. The Mailman had his pad and pencil out, scribbling answers to Lloyd's inquiries about various people, where they were, what they were doing. Then the big question again. The Mailman looked at Kelly and shook his head.

"It's okay. This guy's a friend of mine."

Kelly gave a reassuring smile. "I'm his bodyguard."

The suitcase stood there like the fourth person in the room. The Mailman didn't say anything.

Lloyd got an idea. He went into the kitchen and came back with a little silver box. "You guys want to do a couple of lines?"

The Mailman gummed his. Kelly demurred. Lloyd fetched a bottle of rye and a greasy tumbler. Kelly eyed it. Then, after Lloyd had done his own toot, the Mailman said, "Zomeding do choe you," and opened his suitcase and propped the two paintings on the couch beside him.

Even to Kelly, uncranked, they glowed like gorgeous Technicolor movies.

"Vitz Euww Lane."

"Holy shit. Holy fucking shit." Lloyd was kneeling in front of the couch, face right up against them. "Where did these come from?"

It was easier to understand him now, as he unrolled the narrative of his retirement, the cancer, the part-time job. Kelly flashed on the pill bottle, made him for an addict. The poor guy had never had a chance.

Lloyd was having a different reaction. He beheld the paintings for a long time, then sat back in his chair, exhaled. "You know who John Wilmerding is?"

Head shake on the *no* axis.

"He's the expert on Fitz Hugh Lane. Wrote the book a few years ago. Catalogued every Lane painting and drawing in existence. If these came from Harrison Crowe and the Gloucester library, they're in Wilmerding's book. They're known. No gallery will touch them. No auctioneer. Not in this country, anyway."

The Mailman wasn't getting it. Wasn't wanting to get it.

"They're too good," Kelly interpreted gently. "Too famous. They'd be impossible to fence."

The Mailman burped his disbelief.

"Plus which, you've already taken them across state lines. So it's a federal beef now. Even if I could find a buyer, it'd be pennies on the dollar. Too much risk for the return."

"Lloyd's right," said Kelly again, as gently as he could.

"But you could still get out clean on this if you got in your car right now and put them back where they came from."

Kelly consulted his watch. "What is it, Friday? You got all weekend to fix this, pal."

The Mailman looked like somebody had shot him.

Irene's Type

Gloria opened her door and let in a jangling rush of street noise, followed by Irene Kornecki, all leggy and pert. She introduced herself to Jarkey, sat down, and helped him finish the joint. While they smoked, Gloria enlisted Harry's help in telling the Gallagher story—including his role, which, Jarkey was happy to see, elicited an approving eyebrow arch from Irene.

"Anyway, we're headed uptown to let Daddy know about Kevin. Though it'll probably be Julie who does the talking. I think I need to stay clear of Papa Bear for a while."

"That rotten son of a bitch."

"Daddy?"

"Kevin! We've got to tell Juan and Leo what's going on. The Feds'll be desperate to hang something on them. I don't even think Juan's legal. And poor Lloyd's a drug bust waiting to happen."

Jarkey noted that, while her face was not as beguiling as Gloria's, it gave off a certain boyish sexiness.

"Leo can get hold of Juan." She picked up the phone and dialed his number. They could hear the tinny sound of it ringing and ringing on the other end of the line.

"Try Lloyd," suggested Irene. Contrary to what Lloyd had told Kelly, *everyone* had his number.

More unanswered rings.

"If you don't mind my butting in, those guys aren't the only ones with exposure in this. You both should think about getting your stories together, maybe disappear until you do. Suppose Gallagher and the Feds use your friend's immigration status to turn him? They tell him what to say in return for immunity, then use his testimony to trump up a conspiracy rap on the rest of you." It was a credible effort for a besotted man, who understood that if he wanted to keep up with these women, he'd better do more than ogle them.

"Really, aside from demonstrations and marches, the only thing we ever did was steer cases to Irene," Gloria protested. "All that violent stuff was Kevin's bullshit. And now we know where that was coming from. Nobody ever actually bought into it."

Irene nodded, musing. "Gloria . . ." It came out almost impish, like she was putting her pal on. "Have you seen *The Endless Summer* yet?"

"Yeah." Looking puzzled, but just for an instant.

"Well, maybe he's right. Maybe you ought to take a vacation." The marijuana helped Jarkey see that Irene, too, had something very attractive going on with her eyes—round, calm hazel pools—something she'd doubtless learned from Gloria's dancing slits. Some kind of coded jive they could do with their faces. It seemed, just for an instant, that Gloria was telling Irene, *Nice guy, but not my type,* and Irene was responding, *I don't mind giving him a tumble.* It was all so swift and instinctive that none of them could be sure it had actually transpired.

The telephone rang. The three of them jumped.

Gloria picked it up and said, "Yes," and a second more tentative yes. Then she turned away, saying, "No . . . Oh, shit . . . Yes. I'll be right there." She hung up, staring at them.

"Gloria?"

"Three Mob guys destroyed Daddy's office. They hurt him and Seamster. Daddy's in the hospital with a broken arm."

Fear seeped into the apartment and thickened the air in the room.

Irene said, "This is bad."

"I've got to see him."

The light suddenly seemed very yellow. The three of them, stoned, played hot potato with the feelings they were experiencing. If the Mob was involved, everyone was at risk. They freaked.

Gloria bolted for her bedroom. Harry and Irene could hear her in there, closet door slamming, suitcase snapping, drawers sliding. They each wanted to say something but could not. Then Irene tossed the roach into the ashtray and got up to leave.

Jarkey said, "Wait. I'll drive you. Both."

Irene nodded, sat back down.

Gloria appeared empty-handed. "I changed my mind. No suitcase."

Jarkey got them into the car, and, incredibly, without being assaulted by Mafia hit men. They drove in silence to the hospital on the Upper East Side.

When they got there Jarkey offered to wait. Gloria told him to go ahead and drive Irene home. "I might be awhile with my father and Julie. There's no point dragging you into this."

Jarkey nodded, wished her luck.

Irene took Gloria's place in the passenger's seat. "I guess you know where I live?"

"I guess."

"Want to get a cup of coffee first?"

"Sure."

Better, Yes

The long wait at the hospital calmed Gloria down, gave her time to feel her power returning. Finally she saw her father tottering down the brightly lit hallway. His left arm sported a fresh plaster cast that ended in a pink claw and a plastic bag of meds. Julius Roth had a gentle grip on the other arm. Richard Mundi looked alarmingly frail. She'd imagined the difficulty of telling a pompous, bullying father that, thanks to her, the FBI knew about the heroin he was holding. This was worse. He looked so bad, she wondered whether the news might not kill him.

As his daughter approached, Mundi saw the worry on her face and stood straighter, then smiled. At this moment of crisis there was no one he wanted to see more than her.

Gloria felt his love. She could almost hear him telling her, *Go ahead and do what you need to do. I'd do the same if I were you.* He was receding. She was coming on. That was the natural order of things. His benediction.

"Daddy! Julie told me what happened. It must have been awful."

"Hurt like hell." He realized, to his delight, that the storm wrought by the Street Brothers had cleared the air. All the small-time shit between his daughter and him had fallen away. He loved her, that was all.

He gave her a hug with his good arm and she gave him the air kiss she always did, then pushed away. "Daddy, we've got to talk. There's more to this than you know."

It was late. The hospital coffee shop was closed, but at least the visitors' lounge was empty. Roth got bad coffee from the machine and Gloria told them about Gallagher. How he'd come in and hijacked everything she and Irene had been trying to establish. How she'd gone along at first, deluded. How she'd told Gallagher what she knew about the Newark find, then realized her mistake. How Kelly's man had found out Gallagher was working for the Feds.

"You were right, Daddy. You were right about Kevin. I understand why you hired that detective."

Richard Mundi winced, then was soothed by the thought of Kelly's imminent death. "Fat lot of good being right is doing me."

"Daddy, this is serious."

"You're telling me, sweetie."

Gloria was happy to have energized him. Roth understood it was just the painkillers kicking in. "The sooner we get that stuff back to them, the better for everyone," he said. "We've got hours, not days."

"It's already too late, Julie."

"Boss—"

"Calm down. I'm not talking about selling the stuff. Though I admit, I did have someone lined up in Chicago."

Roth grunted, shot Gloria a look.

"Then I was headed for Spain. Right out of O'Hare on a 707. But not after this." He wagged his cast at them. It wasn't every day you got your wrist snapped by a mushroom. "DiNoto's not going to give us an inch. And now fucking Gallagher's got the Feds in on the deal. Even if I get away clean, you'll be caught up in it. We've got to get rid of that shit. I mean we've got to get ourselves way clear of it."

"The Hudson River," said Roth.

Mundi shook his head.

"The detective," said Gloria, just as her father was having that same thought.

He beamed at her. "Yes, Kelly."

"Funny thing is, I'm pretty sure his sidekick is hanging out with Irene. Right at this moment. Why don't I call him? We'll give him the stuff and tell him to take it to Kelly."

"Then we'll call the Feds and tell them Kelly's got the drugs."

Roth's turn for the nugatory head shake.

"Problem, Julie?"

"Problem? The problem is being dead or in jail. I don't have a problem with transferring that problem to the detective. The real problem is that DiNoto's boys are watching everything we do. That's exactly why they rousted you, boss. To scare you into something like this. We send our guy out of the office with a suitcase and they're on him as soon as he hits the street. Then they find us and kill us." He paused. "I see that as a problem."

"Duly noted."

"Why don't we just call the Feds?"

"There's a reason they call possession 'possession.'"

Mundi and his daughter attempted to discuss the problem further. Then they realized Roth was working on something. They waited to see what he would say. Gloria thought she could guess. Mundi recalled the shabby treatment he'd recently accorded his right-hand man and was searching his limited emotional vocabulary for a proper expression of regret when Roth spoke up.

"Same basic plan, except that I figure a way to get the drugs over to Kelly's without the Mob guys noticing. Then I call DiNoto instead of the Feds. I'll tell him he put the fear in us. I'll tell him we got the word in Newark that it was Kelly who'd found the stuff during the riots, and all we'd wanted to do was sell the information. I won't even tell them to toss his office. That'll be the first place they go."

"You think they'll buy a story like that?"

"What choice do they have? The fact that they left you guys standing means they don't know for sure we're holding it. If they find it on Kelly, we'll look a lot better than we do now."

Gloria sat quietly, taking it all in.

Roth watched her watching and wondered what she saw. "First thing to do is get that stuff planted on our stooge. I'll take care of that. Boss, you need to go the airport right now. Buy a new ticket, then go sit with the customs people, whatever. I doubt even DiNoto's goons would try anything in a public place crawling with cops. Anyway, it'll be obvious you don't have the stuff. You're probably as safe there as you'd be anywhere."

"Except here."

"Well, I guess you could retire to long-term care. Hang out with Murchison."

"I don't think so."

"Gloria, you want to go with him?"

"Well . . ."

"Too dangerous." Mundi patted her knee. "You don't need to be a part of this, honey."

Gloria flushed with relief. Her plans for that evening did not include sitting at JFK with her father. "Daddy, are you sure you're going to be all right by yourself?"

"Of course I am. All I've got to do is get on a plane."

Gloria said, "Okay. Take good care of yourself." But she hesitated, did not leave.

Roth phoned Mossman and sent him over to the Tishman Building, telling him to clean out the safe at Mundi Enterprises, then wait there until Curtis arrived.

Next he called Curtis, the lobby guard. "Curtis, what time do you get off?

"Matthews usually comes in around eleven forty-five."

"For the twelve-to-eight shift, right?"

"Right."

"Fine. Soon as he gets there, scoot up to Mr. Mundi's office. Mossman'll be waiting for you. He'll have something to give you."

"Oh, what?"

"Ten kilos of uncut heroin."

"Far out."

"They're in baggies. Put some in your lunch pail and stuff the rest in your drawers. Then walk over to Fiftieth. I'll be waiting on the corner of Madison in a tan Olds."

"A tan Olds."

"There'll be a couple of grand waiting there with me."

"A thousand a block. Righteous."

Curtis was dark black and weighed two-eighty, an impressive package in his rent-a-cop uniform—and packing heat besides. Roth was certain he'd pass through the midnight streets unmolested; the Mob boys, intent on Mossman, would ignore him after his shift in the lobby was done. Curtis was from Newark, just like Smoot. Roth had gotten him the lobby job, and now he used what he knew about the man to frame the proposition appropriately. No bullshit, high risk, high reward, immediate gratification.

There was nothing to do then but walk Mundi out to the street and put him in a cab. He smiled up at his daughter as she helped him into the backseat.

"Things are going to be different now, sweetie."

"Better, maybe."

"Better. Yes."

Jarkey's Gril

Harry Jarkey, meanwhile, was sitting in the apartment behind the legal office on 116th Street trying to recover from having just gotten his brains fucked out by Irene Kornecki. But he never fully got them back. Not that night, anyway.

After leaving the hospital they'd gone for the cup of coffee, and Jarkey, responding to Irene's out-front energy, wound up telling her about his newspaper career and then, amazingly, about the Julie Christie look-alike and his emotional recovery under Kelly's protection. She'd listened patiently, in a nonjudgmental way, said "Wow" a couple of times. She then explained to him how she and Gloria had met and what they were trying to accomplish relative to the inevitable changes that were about to occur in this country, and how it was just as important to have people working from inside the system as it was to have people attacking it from the outside. He'd nodded, wondering at her unusual sexiness. And of course she'd been receiving all this telepathically, so she simply smiled and said, "Let's go to my place."

To which Jarkey had replied, "Good idea."

Now she was in her robe and he was in his shorts, and she was suggesting that a man with his skills could be a great help. It didn't have to be anything full-time, just a well-placed article every now and then. There might even be the occasional scoop. After all, she *did* deal with some high-profile cases. Jarkey was wondering if they'd get another one in that evening when Gloria called, asked for him, and told him to meet her back at the hospital.

It didn't even occur to him to ask why.

She spotted the black Fairlane before Jarkey saw her and she waved her arms semaphore style until he recognized her and pulled over. She slid in beside him, fresh and excited.

"How'd it go with your father?"

"He's okay, but you'd better call your boss and tell him to get out of town. Daddy and Roth are setting him up to take a fall."

"Kelly?"

"Roth is going to plant the stuff in Kelly's office tonight, then sic the Mafia goons on him. If they find him, they'll kill him."

Jarkey stared at her, speechless, severely conflicted. His former lust-object had apparently been complicit in contriving the murder of his friend and protector.

Gloria read him perfectly. She extended his stunned silence and returned his questioning look with a look of her own—frank, eager, brimming with promise. She squeezed his hand. "Your friend will be safe, Harry. *We're going to get that stash.*"

They drove down to Sammy's, Kelly's most likely hangout, but Kelly was gone. Norbert said he thought the detective had been headed downtown. He handed Jarkey the house phone.

"Lloyd, put Kelly on. I need to talk to him." Even Jarkey had Lloyd's number.

"He left a few hours ago. Where are you? We got a sort of situation here."

"Sammy's."

"Well, he'll probably be back eventually."

"Eventually won't do."

Like all good reporters, Jarkey had a gift for names and contact information. Without a thought he dialed Pepsi's number. Pepsi was a short, dark, vivacious whore of uncertain origin with whom Kelly maintained a "relationship" that baffled everyone who knew them both.

"Yah. Hoo sees?"

"Pepsi. It's Harry. I need to find Kelly."

"Haree! How you?"

"Fine. Fine. Kelly's not there, is he?"

"Ah, Kellee. Dot sweet cookumber. You know he got Clareesa out on bail?"

"Tonight?"

"Oh, lass week maybee."

"I need to talk to him. Do you know where he is?"

"Sure! He at Samee's. So how you doeen? You got a gril yet?"

Jarkey got off as gracefully as he could and gave Gloria a shrug. "I guess we could try his office."

The Plague of Smiling Fishermen

Having polished off half a dozen cherries and the grilled blue-fish special at Sammy's, Kelly ambled back to his office, his head full of images of the Mailman's ravaged face and blasted hopes. He poured himself a shorty and sat in his chair, drowsy. Then he lost touch with the waking edge of himself and a dream filled him.

He was waiting for smugglers who worked on a fishing boat in a seaport town. He had a room upstairs in a tenement by the harbor and when he went down on the street he bumped into a burly, bearded fisherman in a checkered shirt. It was cold. He could see the other man's breath. He wondered if this might be the smuggler and looked up into his face, all bright red cheeks and nose, and the merriest eyes, gay slits under bushy brows, enjoying the joke of an enormous secret. Who cared about smuggling? This was better.

The late-afternoon winter sun made the brick buildings burn orange. Kelly walked around the corner and saw another man approaching. Strangely, this man was identical to the first. Same clothes, red cheeks, laughing crinkles. Then, riding that wave of coincidence, two more, walking together step for step. By the time he got to Main Street there was a steady stream on the sidewalk, all identical fishermen. Kelly looked across the street and it was the same. Legions of merry fishermen, burly and silent and twinkling. Waves of them replicating in doorways and around corners, up from cracks in the sidewalk, out of one another. A plague of smiling fishermen crowding out the rest of the world. That was their joke.

He tried to turn off the street, into a store, but when he opened the door a river of them gushed out and pushed him back to the curb. He could smell the wet wool of their shirts; see the condensed breath glistening like jewels in their red beards. They pushed up close against him, smiling. His arms were pinned. It was difficult to breathe. They were crushing him.

He woke with a start, in his chair, under the lamp, glass in hand. Then he heard the noise that woke him. A key in the door to his office.

Jarkey rushed in followed by, of all people, Gloria Mundi.

Still punchy from the dream, Kelly rose unsteadily to his feet. "Gad, sir. What is the meaning of this?"

"Kelly, this is serious."

"What's she doing here?"

"Better sit back down. It's going to take some explaining."

Gloria broke in. "Harry, we've got to get out of here!"

"On second thought, come with us."

Back in the Fairlane they explained the whole thing in stereo, Jarkey from the driver's seat, Gloria in back. Gloria intended to scare him out of town.

Kelly didn't care for what they had to say. Being lied to was one thing; getting set up to be murdered by enraged Mafia hit men was downright abusive. He sat in silence for a long time, trying to figure out where it'd all gone wrong and how to make it right.

Suddenly he leaned over to Gloria in the backseat. "Your father had a very hard time talking to me about your mother's role in this."

"My *mother?*"

"Don't play cute with me, Sweetheart. I know what's going down here."

Gloria stared at the detective, shocked, as if he'd just slapped her. This man was a complete idiot. He'd do very well for what they had in mind.

Kelly turned to Jarkey. "Get her home. I'm going to need the car for a while."

"I'll bet you're going to need it. What'll it be? Mexico or Canada?" Jarkey imagined Kelly doing just what he would have done. Driving night and day. To someplace very far from Newark, New Jersey.

Kelly shot him a look. "You're thinking small, Jark. That'd be playing right into their hand."

His friend was up to something, but Jarkey didn't want any part of it. A vision of 116th Street was already tugging at him.

"Okay. I don't need to tell you to be careful."

"Thanks, Harry. Be careful your own self. I'll give you a call later, see how you're doing."

Right, thought Jarkey. A call asking me where the car keys are.

Smoot's Doom

Kelly stopped by Sammy's and drank two shots of Wilson's, bang, bang, standing at the bar, working out his plan. Then he marched out the side door and headed up the street to the All Nite Deli where he bought a large black coffee and went to the liquor store across the street for a half-pint of Wilson's. He proceeded to the pay phone on the corner and called Lloyd.

"We got a problem here, Kelly. The Mailman won't take the paintings home."

"That's perfect. Tell him not to worry. I've got a proposition for him that's going to make everything okay."

"You're not hearing me. It's really bad. He won't talk. He won't get off my couch. What do I do with him when Helen comes home?"

"Just keep him there. Do whatever you have to do. I've got a deal going down tonight that'll put everything right."

"I'll try."

It had turned into a pleasant enough evening. Kelly took his coffee and hooch over to Lexington Avenue and stationed himself in a doorway kitty-corner from his building.

The Mob had him in their sights already, or soon would, which meant he'd be a dead man unless he could bring some resolution to the situation. No point dragging Mundi in front of the Newark boss to make him confess. He'd kill the both of them on the spot.

He knew he was right about Agnes Day, but that didn't matter for the moment. It wasn't about her. It wasn't about Gloria either, or Gallagher. The whole thing had been a con from the start. Mundi'd set him up. Hired him so that he'd have someone to dump the heroin on if the Mob got too close. Now the situation was already beyond redemption. He'd have to do the Vietcong thing—disappear into the jungle and commence guerrilla action. It was regrettable. It'd be messy.

One thing for sure—none of those bastards would ever see that smack again.

Presently, a tan Olds pulled up to the front door of his building. Out stepped a burly bald guy with a small suitcase. Kelly recognized him from Mundi's office. He put the case down and fiddled with the lock on the lobby door almost like he was trying to get the right key. In less than two minutes, Kelly noted admiringly, the door was open. Before long he was out again, into the Olds, and gone.

Kelly figured he had a little margin, but he didn't want to waste any time. As soon as the car was around the corner he sprinted across the street and let himself in, heart hammering on the seemingly endless elevator ride up to his office.

The suitcase was on top of a filing cabinet, not even hidden. Kelly set it on the desk and flipped it open.

There sat Smoot's doom—wafting tendrils past Kelly, to Roth, Jarkey, Gloria, Lloyd, Mundi, Mr. D., and the Mailman. Not because it had selected these people or because they wanted it so badly, but simply because of the construction of things. There were no people, no junkies or detectives, just whorls of energy forming and re-forming. And there was no time, no endgame, just gravity sluices between the whorls. No motives, only geometry. And the old Turk's load was not ten plastic sacks of diacetyl morphine sitting in a suitcase, but itself a tendril, tied back through endless iterations to the Promise with the first men who grew and harvested it.

Mekonion, so called by the ancients, locked since Neolithic times in its proprietary arrangement with humans, to whom it offered knowledge of heaven in exchange for its own continuance. Hippocrates called it *opos.* To Galen it was *Opium thebaicum.* Godly purplish flowers in their sacred dance with old men in rippling fields, consuming light, making divine juice. *Papaver somniferum.*

The Promise held until the British got strung out on tea and sent most of their free cash to China in exchange for that invigorating herb. Enter Clive, himself a junkie, and India, where they grew the most lustrous poppies, which the Brits refined and started sending to China in increasing quantities, knowing that once tried, the stuff would create its own demand—"junk," as William Burroughs observed, being the ideal product. One thousand chests of opium in 1767; four thousand by 1790; thirty thousand by the time the first Opium War ripped China open to the West, with missionaries helping to push it in exchange for a chance to spread the Gospel. By the 1870s a third of that nation was addicted and Britain had settled the massive trade deficit caused by its own insatiable craving for Chinese tea. Then a Brit discovered $C_{17}H_{17}NO(C_2H_3O_2)_2$. A German gave the stuff its Heroic appellation—thinking it might be good for curing morphine addiction and—you know the rest.

Kelly snapped the suitcase shut and went down to Lloyd's.

Roth called Mr. D. and ratted Kelly out.

Irene Kornecki let Harry Jarkey back in.

Kevin Gallagher told Agent Spaulding that Gloria's father was holding the stash.

Lloyd and the Mailman did another line.

Mundi's Revenge

Mundi headed for the airport. Hauling his bulk into the cab made his wrist hurt again, so he took a couple more pills.

There were certainly difficulties to be overcome, but in saying good-bye to Gloria he'd felt, for the first time in a long time, the glow of accomplishment. They'd arrived at an essential understanding. Soon DiNoto would be off his back and the highly annoying Kelly would be dead. He hadn't figured out precisely how he'd punish Gallagher, but he reckoned Gloria would be happy to help him there. And Roth, with some careful supervision, would dispose of what was left of Mundi Enterprises. (Kraft and Murchison could go to hell.) So no finders keepers, but he'd make do. He'd sell the house in Westchester and add the proceeds to his Swiss account. Spend a little time on the Costa del Sol, just like he and Agnes used to do. He still had a few Spanish connections. Talk to Franco's people about local business opportunities.

The problem hadn't been that he was getting old—though that was manifestly the case—it was that he'd gotten tired, bored, stale. As the cab sped toward JFK, the image came to him of driving, falling asleep at the wheel for an instant, and being wakened by the noise of the tires on the road's shoulder. He'd gotten control just in time. He was still in the game. He was riding a terrific adrenaline buzz.

As the driver was dropping him off, and he was fishing with his good hand for a twenty, a car screeched to a stop immediately behind them. The commotion attracted his attention. He saw two men get out and approach him. Mundi recognized them as the two who'd destroyed his office that afternoon. He realized they were there to kill him and, with that realization, his heart seized up. God's hand descended into the plane of our daily lives, squeezed his chest, and pulled him back with it into the firmament. A blue jolt shot up Mundi's spine into his brain and he went down on the curb, still clutching the twenty.

As his dying eyes beheld Vince and Woody, frozen in astonishment, his last thought was: "How about *that*, you fucking assholes."

Too Little, Too Late

Irene let Harry back in, but not until Gloria was finished with him. "Give me the keys to Kelly's office." They were standing on Fifteenth Street, just off Union Square, where Kelly'd unceremoniously dumped them. The bars hadn't closed yet, but sleepy sailors were beginning to stagger back to the Seafarers Hotel around the corner. If Kelly had been there, he'd have recognized a few from his dream.

"What for?" Jarkey was getting tugged a lot of different ways. Lust, loyalty, and lucre gleamed in the night.

"C'mon, Harry. You know what for. We've already warned your pal. What happens to him depends on his choices now. But that heroin's sitting in his office, just waiting to be grabbed. Why leave it for the bad guys?"

"It's shit, Gloria. It's poison. No matter where it ends up, it's going to destroy people."

"At least with us some of those losses will be redeemed. Do you have any idea how far even a quarter-million dollars would go?"

"Do you know how much jail time you'd do if you got caught with ten kilos? Think about it!"

"I *have* been thinking, Harry. All those hours of bullshitting in the *foco* I've been thinking there had to be a better way."

"And then, oh Jesus, you're going to be walking around Manhattan in the middle of the night with all that smack? The junkies'll eat you alive."

"Look, I've been on the streets. I've done the tear gas and the dogs and the pigs in their riot gear. That's not the Revolution. That's nothing but cheap thrills. Street theater. This is risk, Harry. Real, honest, calculated risk, with a huge upside. We put that money into legal action and education and we accomplish way more than guns and bombs."

The argument went back and forth, and they finally had to sit down on a bench. Was Jarkey with them or against them?

Jarkey went silent, trying to figure out if helping her get the heroin would be a betrayal of Kelly. She kept at him. They walked. He could've gotten on the subway and left her standing there but, just like in the car, couldn't bring himself to break it off with her. A beautiful rich girl begging him for help—this was more excitement than he'd had in years. Irene might've scrambled his brains, but Gloria still had his imagination. He was a romantic, after all.

She heard the tumbler click, nudged closer to him.

"Let's try it," he said.

No one in front of Kelly's building. No one on the elevator. Jarkey turned the key in the lock to Kelly's office door, reached his arm around, and flicked the light switch.

Silence. The familiar, friendly clutter. Nothing but the usual. No heroin.

Gloria said, "I'll be goddamned."

Jarkey didn't know what to make of that. "Huh?"

"Roth kept the stuff," she told him. "Got it from Curtis and ..."

"I'll be goddamned," he repeated solemnly, happy at not being murdered by waiting thugs, trying his best to honor her perplexity. She was wearing a beguiling mustache of perspiration. "We need to get out of here."

"I need a phone."

They stopped at a booth a few corners away. Gloria called Roth's home number in Forest Hills.

"Julie, what the hell are you doing?"

"What the hell do you mean, 'What the hell are you doing?' *I'm* trying to go to sleep."

"The drugs weren't at Kelly's, as perhaps you knew."

"You little brat. I didn't think you had it in you. You just came from there?"

"A couple of minutes ago." It was odd, the way you got to know people. She could tell from his voice that he didn't have it, either. Not anymore.

"No way DiNoto could've gotten someone there that fast."

"Kelly's got the stuff, then." She turned to Jarkey.

"Don't look at me! You were in the car with us. You know as much as I do."

"You and Kelly can straighten that out later," Roth told her. "We've got a bigger problem now. DiNoto's going to go apeshit when he finds out we're fucking with him. It's going to get messy. You need to disappear."

"What about you?"

"Honey, I'm going to throw some stuff in a bag and get out of here as fast as I can. That's how serious I am. You'd better do the same. If those guys find you, they'll kill you. What's going down now, we don't want to be in their way."

Roth made her copy down the number at which he might be reached in case of serious emergency. Then he hung up, dressed, and threw some things into a bag just like he'd said he would. He was crossing the Tappan Zee when the phone rang back in Forest Hills. The cops were calling to tell him that Mundi was dead.

Gallagher's Dinner

Mossman waited quite a while after Curtis left. He called Matthews down in the lobby a couple of times and there was nothing going on. Eventually he decided it would be better to leave than be trapped in the office. But he was wrong. Vince and Woody waylaid him as he came out of the Tishman Building. After a light pistol whipping, he told them whom he worked for and they made him escort them past Matthews back upstairs. Then Vince went back down and bopped Matthews, and, appropriating his shirt and hat, took his place. There he waited until the Mushroom brought Doc Viera over to open the safe. As he sat, Vince watched the street and thought about nothing, whistling the first bars of some old song over and over.

Viera looked eighty years old, a stick of a man with waxy skin showing well-used blue veins beneath. Everyone said he looked the way he did because he was a cleaned-up drug addict, which had something to do with how he'd learned to do what he did, which he did so well that everyone called him the Doctor. He was only forty-five, and what he did was crack safes. Though Woody wondered if the "Doctor" handle didn't have pharmacological connotations. He'd asked Viera about it once but got no answer.

Viera told Woody that he, Vince, and the Mushroom would be taking care of things there. Woody was to call Mr. DiNoto, who had something else lined up.

DiNoto told him, "I just got a call from Mundi's boy. He claims a PI named Kelly made off with the stuff on the night of the riots."

"Mundi's dead, Mr. D."

"Whaa? You do him?"

"No. A heart attack right there at the airport. No suitcases, no baggage claim ticket. No smack, that's for sure."

"That son of a bitch." DiNoto was definitely pissed at Mundi for dying. "Well, then, maybe this Roth guy was right about Kelly. Anyway, his office is at 509 Madison Avenue. Corner of Fifty-Third. Seventeenth floor. They sounded pretty sure the stuff was there."

"Probably put it there themselves."

"Probably. So toss the place. Get the stuff. Get him and get that Roth guy, and all the little shits that work for him. Mundi has a daughter, doesn't he? Get her, too. Hurt them all. Do what you have to. I'm very tired of all this. These guys are making me look like a chump." It was as much as Woody had ever heard his boss say at once, and it made the hairs on the back of his neck stand up. The old man was unpredictable when he got angry, which was all the more frightening. As he left the Tishman Building, Woody began thinking of horror movies that had truly freaked him out.

It took him ten minutes to demolish Kelly's office. He worked methodically through all the versions of *Frankenstein, The Wolfman,* and *Dracula,* then through the sci-fi films like *Them.* The cabinets went over, the desk upside down. No smack anywhere. Not even a trace. He reported the results to Mr. D., who told him to go back to the Tishman. Heads would be rolling in the morning.

While Woody was remodeling Kelly's office, the warrant finally came down from the judge, who had an early tee time and was predictably annoyed about being wakened in the middle of the night. Spaulding took the warrant and another agent named Voorhees to Gallagher, who'd been cooling his heels in one of the interrogation rooms, reading a magazine, and smoking.

Spaulding waved the paper in his face. "I burned a lot of favors getting this. You're coming with us. If this turns out to be bullshit, I'm gonna make you eat it."

"Coming where?"

"I've got a warrant to search Mundi's office."

"In the middle of the night?"

"We're going through every document in the place and we're not going to be disturbed. If there's a safe on the premises or safe-deposit boxes out there somewhere, we'll just wait till the staff arrives."

Gallagher rolled his eyes, offering his usual contemptuous look. But inside, he felt sick. Spaulding had turned greedy, bumping him out of the catbird seat. "I thought the girl and I were going to steal the stuff so we could hang it on the *foco*."

"That plan's changed, sonny boy. We've got your testimony that she knew about the drugs. When we get the father, we've as good as got the daughter."

They screamed uptown in their unmarked car, scattering startled late-night drivers, then killed the siren as they approached Fifty-Third.

Spaulding pounded on the tall glass door with the stylized 666 logo emblazoned above. Vince waved him off.

"Federal agents," he said, spreading the warrant flat against the glass for Vince to read. "Open up."

Vince rose, tucked his shirt in, and escorted the three men to the elevator. "I'll take you up there myself."

"That won't be necessary," Spaulding told him.

"But I insist," Vince replied, the snout of his pistol pointed right at the soft part of Spaulding's belly.

The bell rang. The elevator door opened. "Going up!" He smiled.

A Suitcase Full of Fitz Hugh Lane

The Mailman seemed catatonic, but what he was doing was waiting. Clarity was now his. Things were simple. It was people who made them seem complex. Here he was with a suitcase full of the simplest proposition in the world and everyone was running around thinking up reasons why it was too complicated. All he really needed to do was wait. Something else would happen and his scheme would be viable once again. For example, here came Kelly with a suitcase of his own.

Lloyd, in an obsessive-compulsive groove induced by whatever they'd been taking, was pacing the floor in front of the couch—doorway to front window, front window to doorway. There'd still been no sign of Helen.

Kelly moved the Mailman's suitcase off the couch and replaced it with his own. Snapped the snaps, flipped the lid, and . . .

"Holy shit. Holy fucking shit." Lloyd's eyes resembled shaving mirrors.

The Mailman made a long breathy noise. Desire. Or agony. Or both.

"Mafia heroin. Uncut. Straight off the boat. It's hot and so are they. Burning the town down."

"Holy shit. Holy fucking shit." Lloyd's ability to express surprise was severely curtailed.

Kelly grabbed the Mailman by both shoulders, establishing eye contact. "We're putting this in your car," he said. "In the driver's door panel. Right now. When there's nobody on the street. Then you're getting in that fucking car and driving. You're not stopping until you're home. Lloyd's going with you. You'll take the paintings back to the museum, and Lloyd's going to reacquaint himself with Gloucester's criminal element. We'll sell the shit off the Gloucester waterfront, split the proceeds, and be gone before the Mob guys can figure it out."

"Wrong about that one, Kelly old boy. There's no way on God's green earth I'm getting into a jalopy full of stolen art and heroin."

"Don't be an idiot. This is the chance of a lifetime. The Mailman gets a fresh start, and you and I make some dough on the deal. Things'll be hot for me in this town. But you're clean. Nobody will connect you with this. Nobody even knows about the Mailman."

"I'm not an idiot, Kelly. That's why I'm not getting in that car. Just like with the paintings, only worse. Too much risk, too insufficient a reward."

"Oh, for Christ's sake—"

The Mailman spoke for the first time. "Lloy's right." Then he wrote it out on the pad. "I'll take it back myself. I don't give a shit. I got nothing to lose."

Kelly had to admit it sounded just as good that way. The Mailman wasn't likely to double-cross them. He didn't have any contacts. He'd get himself killed if he tried to fence the shit off. He'd probably dip a little off the top, but who cared?

The detective shrugged at Lloyd. *What do you think?* And Lloyd started thinking. It was hard for him and it took a while. Kelly could almost hear him grinding through it, like trying to start a car that'd sat in the driveway all winter. He resumed pacing, then he began talking.

"It might work. We'd have to break it up into smaller loads. And we'd probably have to go partners with Reardon—but that could be done. It'll just take time, is all. We can't get greedy. We'll have to go slow. And we'll be settling for pennies on the dollar. But considering our investment, it's still a good deal. Or we could cut Reardon out and step on it ourselves. But then we'd be in the retail business, which would not be a good idea for any of us."

"What about this guy Reardon? Suppose he gets ideas?"

"What's he gonna do? I make a trip to Gloucester every month and he thinks I'm diverting the shit from some factory in East Harlem. He takes what I've got and adds it to whatever's going onto the street that week. It's my risk, not his. He'd never figure the Mailman in this, not in a million years."

"So the Mailman holds the stash?"

"That's the way it's got to be."

The Mailman nodded his assent.

They all went down to the street. Kelly and the Mailman stood in front of the Mailman's car while Lloyd popped the panel and stacked the bags inside, leaving room so you could still roll the window down. He replaced the panel and set the suitcase with the paintings in the backseat. Then they all had one last toot and Kelly and Lloyd watched the Mailman head over to the East River Drive.

Gallagher and the Feds

U p in the Tishman Building Mossman was having a rougher time of it. He heard the muffled thump from inside Mundi's office and knew the weird-looking guy had gotten the safe open. When they didn't find what they were looking for, they'd beat him until he told them where it was. Then they'd kill him. He resolved to tell them everything he knew immediately. Get it over with. Just at that moment, however, Vince pushed the Feds and Gallagher into the reception room where Woody and the Mushroom were holding him. Vince handed Spaulding's warrant to Woody, who read it and said, "Well, well." It was getting to be quite a party.

Then Doc Viera emerged from Mundi's office, coughing slightly, and Vince and Woody went to see what was in the safe. Mossman gritted his teeth. Vince came out and smacked him on the side of the face with his gun. It happened so fast, Mossman didn't even have time to flinch.

He went down like a tree, then got to his hands and knees. "The guard. The black guy down in the lobby . . ." His mouth was filling with blood so fast he had to stop and spit it out. "He took the shit out of here while you were waiting for me." More blood. "Roth planted it in Kelly's office. You're supposed to find it there." He crawled against the desk, holding his head, waiting for the shot.

It never came. Vince and the Mushroom wanted to off the newcomers right there. But Woody didn't like the idea of killing federal agents before they'd recovered the heroin. It would draw too much heat. Meanwhile, Gallagher had started screaming, crying, telling them he was no Fed. No pig, no way. He sang his jail time like an aria. He was one of them, he swore. The Feds were blackmailing him to spy on a bunch of college kids.

Vince and Woody were momentarily taken aback by this performance. Doc Viera told them to use Spaulding's gun to shoot Voorhees and Spaulding, Voorhees's gun to shoot Gallagher, and then to put Spaulding's gun in Gallagher's hand to get his prints on it. Gallagher was crying. Spaulding or Voorhees, one, shat his pants. Vince and Woody got a whiff and looked at each other. That happened occasionally. It was unfortunate. Robbed a man of his dignity. They locked the three men in a broom closet off the reception room and returned to the business of Mossman.

Woody grabbed a fistful of his hair and yanked his head up hard. "This guy Kelly. The PI. Got any ideas?" So Mossman described him, wracking his brain for details, sufficiently terrorized by now to have given up his mother had they asked for her. Then he remembered Sammy's Undersea Lounge.

But Sammy's was closed by the time they got there, so they reported to Mr. D. and went uptown for a little shut-eye. It had been a busy evening.

For some reason they didn't kill Mossman. Just left him in a heap by the side of the desk. He went in and out of shock for a few hours. Came to around dawn, roused by the muffled shouting coming from the closet. He thought for a moment about letting them out, then remembered who they were and just went home. The cops didn't arrive until later that morning. It had gotten pretty bad in there by that time.

Hot Town, Summer in the City

The next day came in bright and warm. The brown bubble over the city had finally broken and the rain seemed to have cleansed the air. The Street Brothers and Mr. Fungu tooled down the West Side Highway in Woody's fine Lincoln, happy to be alive. Vince had WKRC on the radio. They all preferred jazz, even the Mushroom, who was watching the boats on the river, smiling. Woody started thinking of famous bandleaders who'd started in other bandleaders' bands, but there were too many. Then he wondered if he could link them all in some kind of genealogy. Vince was whistling softly, waiting for another song to come to him.

They got off at Fourteenth and went down to Gloria's. Vince double-parked and Woody jimmied the door right in broad daylight. It was amazing, the things you could do if you were cool enough about it. The Mushroom slammed through into Gloria's apartment, but she was long gone. Woody performed the requisite search and came up empty.

Then over to Eighth, back up to Twenty-Third, and across to Third Avenue, all restaurants, watch repair shops, dry cleaners, shoemakers, butchers, and delis, gay and teeming in the sun. Up through Murray Hill with its stylish deco building fronts, and past the looming Queensboro Bridge. Vince actually found a parking place on Lex a block down from Sammy's. They went in to use the men's room and the assistant bartender told them when Norbert would show up. They got coffee and sandwiches and sat in the car listening to music, windows rolled down, enjoying the air, waiting. Eventually, when the time came, they went in and slammed Norbert against the wall and he gave them Lloyd. Easy, boys. No trouble.

They drove down to Lloyd's. By this time it was early rush hour and the drive took longer than they liked. However, everything worked out perfectly. Just as they were parking across the street from Lloyd's, his front door opened.

Mossman's description of Kelly was fresh in Vince's mind. He said, "That'll be the dick."

Woody said, "Will you look at that getup? Guy must buy his clothes at the PI store."

Kelly was stepping into the beautiful evening, having spent the day sleeping off the crank he'd done with Lloyd the night before. Lloyd was gone when he woke, probably out on his rounds. So Kelly strolled out for a cup of coffee, leaving his hat and gun behind, busily trying to remember where he'd put his car, wondering where Helen might have been all night and if the Mailman had made it home.

The Mushroom came up behind him and enveloped him. The Lincoln squealed up to the curb and before he could finish gulping back the breath Mr. Fungu had squeezed out of his lungs, Kelly found himself in the backseat with the big guy, a gun in his ribs.

The guy's eyes were dead. Kelly didn't even fantasize about making a move on him.

They drove around the block a few times. Presently Woody appeared on the street and hopped in. "Nothing up there. The other one must've seen us on the street and beat it out the fire escape."

"What now?"

"Let's take him uptown and call the boss."

It was an endless ride, up and up through stop-and-go traffic, into the 200s on the Hudson River side, to the wilds of Riverdale Park. Kelly had plenty of time to analyze this latest evolution. Saw it was the culmination of a pattern that had begun to form with the German and the trannie, when he forced the issue and knocked himself off the wave. Then the mistake with Mundi. Then these guys. The entire situation had drifted from its path. Somewhere, off in the woods, down by the river, Kelly heard a train rumble through the gathering dusk—all the innocent bustle and motion of normal life unreachable. Beyond him. The driver kept whistling something. He'd whistle, stop, start it over again. An old pop tune from the fifties. Kelly could almost place it. No timing, no motivation. Mindless. Eerie. Menacing. He felt as flat as the hard blue sky.

The car pulled up to a wrought-iron gate in a whitewashed wall topped with black spikes. Vince got out and opened the gate, then drove the car down to a garage underneath a massive villa of a house. They dragged Kelly upstairs and put him in a wooden chair in front of a big table. He could see the round fluorescent light tube on the ceiling of the kitchen across the hall, and a warm orange wall. He thought of Aunt Kay's kitchen, and of cookies. It smelled damp, a little mildewed, as if the house hadn't been lived in lately. He could feel the two heavies on either side of him tensing for action. The third, the monster, wiped his nose and looked at him as if he were lunch.

The one on his left said, "This is going to hurt us more than it hurts you."

Kelly didn't believe him. "I'll talk," he said, trying to figure out how much to say, what would be plausible, how he might make his move if one were to be made.

"That's right," the man said. The big guy slapped him halfheartedly, just hard enough to knock him off his chair.

"Let's get him down in the cellar," Vince said. "This is going to make a mess."

Vince and Woody picked Kelly up like a ventriloquist's dummy and dragged him into the hall. Kelly lashed out with a hard right cross, but being held by his armpits three inches off the floor limited his effectiveness.

Then everything went black. Kelly knew the monster had given him a tap on the noggin from behind. Probably'd gotten nervous about the fight he was putting up. That was all right. Like being under ether, they can't hurt you when you're unconscious. Not, mused Kelly, that he enjoyed being hit. It was simply the lesser of two evils. His body went limp. His shoulders slipped through muscular fingers. He slumped to the floor.

It took him the length of that thought, lying there in the comfortable darkness, to realize that the only thing shut off was the lights. The electricity had failed. Nobody had, in fact, knocked him unconscious.

"Vince! You got him?"

He bellied to the wall and wriggled away from the voice. The other voice answered it.

"He's on your side. I can hear him crawling."

Just a few feet ahead of him Kelly saw the dim rectangle of a window. Double swinging sashes about waist high, with diamond shapes leaded in the glass. He dove for it. A lighter snicked on, followed by a muzzle flash.

Dig We Must

At 10:13 that evening a surge of electricity flowed into the Northeast power grid at Cornwall, Ontario, in a direction opposite the normal flow for that hour. Technicians at the Richview control center in suburban Toronto spotted the reversal and, knowing it would seriously damage their distribution equipment, pulled switches that isolated their district from the international network of electrical transmission lines. Toronto blacked out at 10:16.

A massive break had occurred in the circuit somewhere along the U.S.-Canadian border, and the system was compensating by drawing power from other lines in the grid. But the demand on these other lines was too great. They also shorted, tripping more relays, drawing on still other lines, and passing the power drain along in a sort of cascading domino effect.

The surge swept down New York State and moved into parts of Massachusetts and Connecticut. At 10:25 a worker on duty in the Consolidated Edison control center on Manhattan's West Side was monitoring a flow of 300,000 kilowatts from upstate. As suddenly as in Richview, the flow reversed, draining one million kilowatts from nine New York area generating stations. Automatic safety switches tripped, throwing the city into darkness.

The computer-monitored system had been designed primarily to meet the periodic surges in demand for electricity in the northeastern United States. Theoretically, power generated in Canada could light lights in Washington, DC. The way it worked out, however, a break near Niagara Falls was able to extinguish lights as far away as Philadelphia.

President Johnson ordered the FBI and the Defense Department to report on the possibility of sabotage or covert invasion. A memo to the chairman of the Federal Power Commission instigated a simultaneous investigation by that body.

At eleven thirty p.m. the director of the United States Office of Emergency Planning told the president that there'd been a short circuit in the cable of the Niagara Mohawk power system. The Niagara Mohawk Company, which had restored power to its own customers more than an hour before, pointed out that power could not have been restored if there'd been a break in the cable. The company's executive vice president said, "There was no repair crew out because there was nothing to repair."

The United States Office of Emergency Planning replied that its information had come from the Boston Edison Company. A spokesman for the Boston facility denied this, saying, "We're not in a position to tell anyone where the failure is because we don't know." The dean of Engineering at Carlton University in Ottawa came to the conclusion that the circuit had broken on the U.S. side of the border. An officer of the Ontario Hydroelectric Commission seconded this opinion, saying he was virtually certain the break had occurred in the 345,000-volt line maintained by the New York State Power Authority. However, the general manager of the New York body maintained that all his company's lines were intact.

Such considerations aside, there was no electricity anywhere in New York City and environs. Tens of thousands of people were stuck on darkened subways, with thousands more stranded on electric trains of the New York Central and New Haven lines, and the Long Island Railroad. Auto traffic speed on the city's major arteries averaged three miles per hour. Citizens rescued their stranded fellows, pedestrians volunteered to direct traffic, people guarded shops against looting, and a vast majority of residents maintained a calm spirit of cooperation. The sudden, overarching stillness fostered a sort of ethereal communion.

Being a student of the media, Harry Jarkey understood that during the power outage the only effective mass communication was radio. Within minutes of the initial failure, stations improvised emergency hookups and activated generators. People stuck in traffic or their apartments had nothing better to do during the time of crisis than flick on their car or transistor radios and listen. Cousin Brucie's manic patter was shoved aside in favor of broad, soothing tones.

Jarkey recalled Marshall McLuhan's view that electronic circuitry was just an extension of the human nervous system. Perhaps, during the blackout, New York City's electronic web performed in a way analogous to the neural functions of the human body. With its more sophisticated systems knocked out, the city/body lapsed into a comatose condition. It kept itself together only on the most fundamental levels. Each citizen within earshot of a radio acted as a single nerve ending, responding to the messages of bemused calm that flooded the airwaves.

Julius Roth, on the other hand, believed that a different sort of electricity—the current of fear—provided the energy that held the city together. The specter of anarchy was never far from the surface. The apparent cooperation was controlled hysteria, the good cheer a sort of gallows humor. The citizens acted as they did to fend off a deeper, more permanent darkness.

Lloyd Chamberlain would have explained to whomever was in his vicinity that the brain part of the city's body had seized up.

From Norbert's point of view it was just a question of habit. The hardships imposed by the blackout differed only in degree from the difficulties to which people had long been accustomed. All the myriad frustrations and delays they encountered each day were gathered in a single mighty stoppage of energy. Everyone that evening had the same problem. And if, as so often happened in normal times, people were lost, stuck, or out of luck, at least this once they had the satisfaction of knowing why. Because the goddamned power was out.

Beyond that, not even the chairman of the Federal Power Commission, or the director of the United States Office of Emergency Planning, or even the president of the United States himself, could explain.

Still, Irene Kornecki wondered, if it were true that the blackout forced people to work together, how much would freedom from the pervasive, numbing, electrical massage increase their ability to work with themselves? How much would a year without electricity enhance civilization?

The power grid was the envy of the old Turk's load. Everyone was strung out on it.

Glory Train

Kelly rolled through the window, head and neck hunched under the shoulder of his sport coat. Glass shattered and the wood flew into splinters, then the coat flapped around his ears as he tumbled through space.

He decided that, when he got rich, he'd hire somebody who looked exactly like him. He'd teach this double how to talk like him, how to act like him, and how to sign his name. Every day he'd load up the double with a miniature tape recorder and camera, and send him out on the streets. The double would be the one who'd yawn through meetings with clients, and when he was done with them he'd step lively to avoid being eaten by the sharks who swarmed around him. He'd fend off each day's army of backstabbers and con men, being careful not to make any enemies. He'd run out of gas on the highway and stub his toes and spill his soup for his boss, the original, who would sleep late each morning, read the world's newspapers over a leisurely brunch, play a little squash or chess, take a shower, and sip fifty-year-old Scotch till the double stopped off at the end of each day with a full report. Then he'd pass the night in the company of beautiful women. If the women gave him trouble he'd call the double back. The way his life had been going lately, he felt as if he were the double, taking falls for a Kelly he never saw.

The ground surprised him. He hadn't been expecting it so soon. His knees buckled and he rolled onto his side. A jolt of pain shot up through the old, bad ankle. Twelve feet over his shoulder the window framed someone's silhouette. Then a flashlight beam illuminated the ground in front of him. He flattened himself against the wall under the window, shimmied to the corner of the house, and broke for the woods at the edge of the yard. The flashlight caught him then, and gunshots exploded behind him. What would the neighbors think?

"Back here! I've got him!"

Kelly begged to differ.

The ground sloped down on the other side of the trees, but the going was tough. This part of the riverbank had grown into the kind of wilderness that exists only in urban areas: a dense, dirty tangle of invasives and outlaw shrubs growing up through washing machine carcasses and gutted refrigerators. He struggled past the trash and, by the dim moonlight, came upon the barest trace of a path, more traveled by rats and raccoons than humans. Branches slapped him; vines clawed his legs as he bulled his way down toward the river. Finally he was forced to pause, gasping for breath. The darkened hulk of the house loomed behind him. He'd come less than a quarter mile, though it felt like ten times that distance. The flashlight winked and waved at the top of the bank as his pursuers descended.

Ahead of him were the railroad tracks, and beyond them the black glint of the Hudson. He knew he'd have a chance if he could make it to the river. Across the water, from atop the Jersey Palisades, two emergency beacons twinkled a message of safety. He ran for them with all he had.

He didn't have much. Worse, the distance to the water increased as he went on, and his bad habits overhauled him. Fluids gurgled up from his stomach and a gummy deposit accumulated at the back of his mouth. Waste products churned through his body where blood should have been. He could hear cursing and crashing behind him. He tried to increase his pace, but his legs had stopped taking orders.

He saw the shape of the branch that had fallen across the path, but he couldn't bring his lead foot to step over it. His shoe hooked neatly around it and the rest of him sped forward, plowing a six-foot furrow. His head came to rest against a rusting wheel rim.

He gathered himself, drove forward, and fell a second time, gaining a body length. He picked himself up, tried to run, and fell— again and again, deeper into a haze of pain and fear. Nothing was broken. In a few days he'd be fine. Right now he was counting his time in minutes. At this rate, he was only saving them the trouble of carting his body to the river.

Kelly stumbled into the ditch of sewer water beside the train tracks, wanted to huddle there, curl up, slip beneath the mud like a turtle, and not come up until spring. The flashlight beam was closing in behind him. His ankle didn't hurt anymore. He wallowed across the ditch and clambered up the embankment, rolling across the tracks so as not to give them a profile to shoot at. Soon nothing would hurt, ever. As he got to the other side he looked toward his feet and saw an incredibly brilliant light bearing down. His death. A warming, pleasurable surge swept through him. He stood, in the rush of brightness and noise, to meet his end.

The stubby switchyard diesel huffed past at a labored pace and Kelly unthinkingly threw himself onto the utility car that rolled along behind it, snuggling down amid jackhammers and compressor hoses. It was, he thought, so strange and weird to die. Nothing like he'd imagined it. He pulled his coat around him and wished he were back at Sammy's.

The Getaway

Gloria knew Roth wasn't scared. He didn't *get* scared. His hasty departure was simply a sensible move, one she should emulate.

She took a cab up to the Westchester house, did a little packing of her own, then blasted off in the Starship—a black, two-door Olds F-85 with the V-8 engine and a jet-age instrument panel. Her father had bought the car for her and at first she'd hated it. But in fact it was exactly her style—fast and understated—and now she bonded with it as never before. She made Rhode Island as the sun was coming up, and New Hampshire by mid-morning, turning on a whim down a small coastal road that wound east to Hampton Beach, then north over a humpy wooden bridge into the lovely little backwater of Wallis Sands. There was a restaurant called the Lobster Pot next to the creek, a parking lot paved with clamshells, and a rambling old two-story house with apartments on both sides, up and down, front and back. A sign said VACANCY. It seemed a good place to lay low for a spell. She went in to investigate.

A deeply tanned woman with ropey muscles and steel-wool hair came to the door. Gloria, giving her voice just the right amount of girlish trepidation, inquired about the vacancy and was promptly installed in the front apartment for a week. Cash changed hands in advance at Gloria's insistence. She brought in her bag, stretched out on the freshly made bed, and listened to the slap and rush of surf across the road. It smelled faintly of summer cottage mildew, reminding her of beach stays from childhood.

She thought about Daddy and their long struggle. How seeing him hurt in the hospital had so suddenly changed her feelings for him but *not* her determination to get her hands on the contraband. She thought, too, about Irene and Harry, and the stash's so-called rightful owners. She and Harry had missed grabbing it, probably just by minutes. But they were still alive and safe, and now Kelly had the stuff, which was almost as good. All she had to do was hang tight, keep her eyes open, and be ready to make her move when the time came. The family in the apartment next door was getting ready to go to the beach, and the children were making happy, excited noises, sending her drifting back again to memories.

When she woke it was late afternoon and she felt as fresh and clumsy as a newborn. She went out on the porch and sat, inhaling the soft, fragrant air. The woman came out of her office and sat in the chair next to Gloria's. Her name was Maddy. Her husband was the burly fellow hauling lobster pots out of a tar vat; his name was Harold. He was a plumber over at the Wentworth Hotel, but he was also a lobsterman. She, Maddy, baked pies. Gloria told Maddy she went to school in New York and was taking a little break. Maddy had the strangest ocean-colored eyes. Gloria could feel their pull.

"My boyfriend . . ." she murmured. "We broke up."

Maddy clucked sympathetically.

Presently they strolled across the parking lot to the restaurant and Maddy showed her around—fryolator, steamer, grill, picnic benches. It was all spotless. Maddy had a pet seagull named George, in honor of her first husband who, she believed, had come back as this bird. He'd had a stroke that crippled his left side and another that killed him. The bird showed up a while later, half dead, with a broken left leg and a damaged wing. Once she'd nursed him back to health he'd never left. Maddy stood on the restaurant deck that overlooked the creek and screeched "JAWGE!" almost like a seagull herself, and tossed a bit of pie in the air. George swooped out of nowhere and gobbled it on the fly.

Gloria ordered strong black coffee, a lobster roll in a toasted hot dog bun, and a piece of Maddy's heavenly blueberry pie. Late-afternoon marsh grass perfumed the air. Where would a guy like Kelly go with a suitcase full of heroin?

It had to be Lloyd, Kelly's own private stool pigeon and nose-candy connection. So maybe she could get Helen Chamberlain in on the deal. There was a pretty tough cookie. She'd dealt with Lloyd and his bullshit all those years. Maybe she was tired enough of him to help put the proceeds to a more positive use.

After dinner Gloria walked half a mile down the road to Philbrick's General Store and poked around the sleepy, sandy place, chockablock with fly swatters, hula hoops, mousetraps, bins of sneakers, and the most comprehensive display of penny candy she'd ever seen. If the stash wasn't at Lloyd's, Harry would find out from Kelly where it was and lead her to it. Then, who knew? She could mobilize Leo and Harry, maybe even Julie, to get the drugs back from Kelly. Or maybe they'd go partners with him.

At six thirty p.m. she went to the phone booth out front and called, as they'd arranged, the number in New York at which Irene took her calls from fugitives. Gloria gave her the New Hampshire pay phone's number and Irene called her back.

"Did you get out of town all right?"

"Fine. No problems. It's going to be a mellow week. Any sign of DiNoto's guys?"

"Leo stopped by your place. He said it had been destroyed. Must've been them."

"What about Juan?"

"We got him to Montreal."

"And you?"

"I don't like any of this."

Gloria lifted a page from Roth's book—full disclosure jujitsu. "I know you don't like it. But if I don't do something, that drug money will just go to the Mafia. I want it for our work. Give it a chance to redeem itself."

"It's tainted, Glo."

"As if our brothers and sisters haven't been tapping drug funds in the struggles in Latin America and North Vietnam. Money's money. It's what you use it for."

A long conversation ensued. It took everything Gloria had to win Irene over. In the course of the argument she discerned that her friend had gotten serious about Harry Jarkey. Gloria deployed this information to gain Irene's conditional acceptance.

"So you and Harry have been talking?"

"He says he wants to help."

"Oh, he'll be helping, all right."

"Meaning what, exactly?"

"Kelly's already got the stash. Maybe Harry leads us to it."

"How happy do you think he'll feel when he finds out he's being used?"

"He's in with us already. With you. Why don't you ask him how he feels?"

"Come on, Gloria. He wouldn't shaft his detective buddy."

Irene was losing it, Gloria thought. But all she said was, "So maybe Kelly comes in with us, too. Maybe we hire him. Maybe Harry makes him see it's the right thing to do. Anything could happen. It's still evolving."

Walking back to Maddy's after they'd hung up, Gloria thought hard. There were so many possibilities, and she had to be open to all of them. Considered that way, though, it quickly became exhausting. So, with the beautiful certainty of innocence, she refused to think of it that way any longer. She tried to read a little more of *The Confessions of Nat Turner* but was fast asleep by the time the blackout hit Manhattan.

One More for the Road

Blackness passed into dreams of suffocation and falling from high places. It was funny, the ideas you got. Kelly knew he was dead, traveling through dimensions to begin life in a new form, possibly continuing the same life in other realms. Each jolt was the passage of a universe. He had perished and come back in a piece of metal. He was a molecule of the Triborough Bridge. The roar and clatter around him was the noise of others just like him. Molecules, all of them. How long would this last? How long had it lasted?

He sat up. A dull pain rose from the base of his spine and came to rest between his ears. Molecules didn't have ears.

He was on a train.

In a tunnel. Under the Hudson to Jersey.

As the diesel came out of the tunnel and moved slowly into a yard full of tracks and cinders, Kelly rolled off the flatcar and clambered with little difficulty over a chest-high concrete wall. Apparently the ankle hadn't been hurt so badly. Fear had cramped it up, was all. He walked down the street toward the river with hardly a limp.

Except the river wasn't there.

The world was dark. Apartment buildings stood against the night sky like thunderclouds. There were no traffic lights, no street-lights, no lighted store windows, no neon signs over restaurants, no floodlights under movie marquees. Garish automobile headlights bounced off walls at street level and lit the heights with a reflected, dreamlike glow.

Kelly stood in a daze, leaning into the same tumbling dizziness that marked those first morning moments after a night's drinking. Then he blinked the scene into place. The train had gone down the west side rather than under the river. He was in the city.

People moved up and down the street, headed for dinner or carrying groceries. All proceeded as if they had somewhere to go. As if it weren't pitch-black everywhere. A glow of alcohol emanated from a bar. Kelly went in. It was stuffy, with candles in beer bottles on the bar casting a dim, claustrophobic light. He ordered a double shot of Wilson's and a beer. The man beside him was talking to himself in a quavering voice. Just as Kelly was finishing his double the man turned to him and said, "You stink." Kelly moved down the bar.

A transistor radio next to the whiskey bottles blatted out good cheer. Everybody was keeping half an ear open for the news. There was no news. The whole world was dark and nobody knew why, but there was nothing to worry about. It was 10:56. They played "Twilight Time" and a drunk began to sing.

The bartender stood before him, displaying a stern expres-sion arranged around a nose that had been broken once or twice. "Another shot, huh? And a beer," Kelly told him.

The man leaned across the bar and talked out of the corner of his mouth, more confidential than tough. "Listen, bud. Some of the customers are complaining."

"Huh?"

"The smell, you know?"

As a matter of fact, Kelly did smell something. Something sweet and slightly rotten, with a hint of steaming viscera. Something he'd soaked up in the ditch by the railroad tracks. It was ripening in the warm air.

"I stepped into a sewer. Can't even get home to change. Isn't that something?"

"Sure." The bartender took a bottle of Wilson's off the shelf and waved it at the end of the bar. "Mind stepping down by the men's room?"

Kelly did as the man suggested. It was less crowded there, and smelled as much of Pine-Sol as he did of sewer. A dead candle stub sat in an ashtray. The bartender set a glass beside it and poured another double. "No hard feelings, huh? This one's on the house."

Kelly downed it and pulled a soggy dollar out of his pocket. "Here. Buy yourself one."

The bill left an oily spot on the counter when the bartender picked it up. He wiped the spot away and poured them both another. On the house.

The Bridge

Lloyd hadn't planned on making one last suicidal train wreck of a speed run; it just turned out that way.

He and Kelly had done a few more toots after seeing the Mailman off, then gone up to the Zebra on First Avenue still sky-high from the rush of their giddy bullshit plans. Later, back at Lloyd's place, Kelly began to crash. Lloyd fed him a Nembutal, put him to bed, then wandered up to the Brooklyn Bridge in hopes of hearing the badass sax player rumored to hang out there, spinning his wild soliloquies into the night. He thought about Hart Crane and Walt Whitman, and, in the absence of any manic music, about doing another toot. Then another.

Dawn was gorgeous as it spread out before him—*his* dawn, opening like Helen in the old days. Oh, the rotten, vile bitch. Where *was* she, anyway? He commenced a heated conversation with her in his head, in the course of which he remembered she was at a Zen retreat in Vermont for a few days, which was why she wasn't home. Or was it?

He'd seen so little of her lately. He'd sensed she had the hots for Kelly. Why was he putting up with *that*? The conversation moved away from Helen, turning into a spirited debate among himself and the various sub-units of that self—angry Lloyd, righteous Lloyd, Lloyd the victim—made manifest in his over-chemicalized brain. Answering the voices out loud, he shuffled the bridge's length and back. Later he took part in an actual argument in a deli over spilled coffee and the payment for his egg sandwich.

Returning home for some downers to ease him through this increasingly troubled end of his adventure, he found Kelly passed out on the couch. He got distracted, did more speed—instead of downers—then became furious with himself as it hit, realizing he was losing control of the day. Then increasingly furious at the world in which this whole fucked-up mess was taking place—Kelly snoring all the while behind him—he conceived of a mission to score some mescaline, certain it would be an excellent antidote for what, he could see, was only, after all, a minor disturbance. Like taking a few aspirin when you have a cold. Gulping calming breaths, he put this sudden inspiration up as a shield against the voices that swarmed around him like a cloud of gnats.

The serious bugs didn't arrive until later. Not until after he'd gotten in the fight with Bruno, who had no mescaline to offer, but with whom he did a few lines of coke. The problem was it turned out to have been bad shit, cut with something searing and horrible and causing him to threaten Bruno's life. Bruno got his back up and his knife out, and this was scary. Frightened, suddenly—crying, for Christ's sake, because everything was jolting in and out of blackness—he started to freak when the bugs tunneled into the skin on his forearms. He knew that if they reached his brain, it was going to be a very bad scene.

Somehow he made it home again, dodging menace at every corner. The moment he opened the door he realized the place had been trashed. He grokked right away that the bad guys had done this, that they were after the smack. They'd probably nabbed Kelly. Had he been asleep on the couch when they showed up? Where was Helen? He knew he needed downers. Took a slug of the rye he'd gotten out for Kelly the night before. Retched. The bugs were all over him now.

All of a sudden his clothes caught fire. This got him to the tub, where he furiously ran the water, got in, and began scrubbing at the bugs. Then the bath went cold and he pulled the plug. But before he could reach for his towel he had a seizure—though what it actually felt like was the deepest sensation of cold, as if his core had been injected with slushy ice. He was overcome with violent shivers, teeth-clacking shudders, and he hunched in the fetal position there, in the tub, just trying to take his next breath.

Which was when the power went off. The blackout plunged him and his speed-wracked psyche into a darkness so profound, he could feel it pressing down upon him, then *into* him. It evacuated whatever had been there before, replacing it with pure emptiness. Against which the thought of the Mailman, the heroin, Kelly, the Mafia, his ruined apartment, his life with Helen—the whole panorama suddenly seemed no more than an illusion. A mental trick. In a piercing, soul-rending insight it came to him: THIS was the true reality. He was the brain. This was the jar. *He was the brain in the jar.*

He whimpered, empty and trembling in the bottom of the tub, too weak to resist. He was the receptacle, what it all was rushing into. All the signals from the other computers, the ceaseless clatter of money being transferred, of airliners being routed, stocks traded, trains switched. Endlessly, with no rest, ever. The orders from 'Nam, calling in fire, dispatching more stainless steel choppers.

The mangled bodies, oozing brains. Firebombed babies. Napalmed Cong. Grunts in death agonies. Saigon whores in micro-miniskirts freebasing, going up in flames. It was the drugs. The drugs were the circuits pinning him here. Now he understood the trap he was in, the true nature of the jar. He writhed in his tub. The core of him was twisted so tight, and it kept getting tighter. It hurt so bad. He was so thirsty.

The Bank Street Dream

It was just past midnight. The blackout still held Manhattan in its grip, but traffic was beginning to clear up. Kelly, fueled by half a dozen shots of Wilson's, was walking again, pounding down Hudson. Where to go? A passing headlight illuminated the street sign for Bank and he took a left. He was riding the current now.

Gloria's place, south side of the street. Flash of sitting in the car with Jarkey, outside the apartment, Jark explaining things. That seemed a long time ago. Then it didn't seem like time at all, just jumps. He went up the stoop and stood at the building's main door. First this reality, then the next, then the next. The door was mangled around the lock. Almost looked right, but . . . He pushed against it and it opened. Same with Gloria's apartment door. Someone had been there before him.

He held his Zippo aloft, scanning first her big front room, then the hallway, bedroom, bathroom, and kitchen. No bodies, but the place was a wreck. Just as the lighter started to burn his hand, he spotted two candles amid the kitchen mess. He lit these, stuck them on plates. If you thought about it, a proper search required method. It didn't look as if that had been part of the game plan here, though. He suddenly flashed back to his captors placidly driving him to where they could torture and kill him. He understood he was now safer here than he would be walking around.

In the bathroom he cleaned himself up until the hot water was gone from the tank. He'd come through pretty well, with only a few cuts on his shoulders and right forearm. His coat was shredded, but overall, he wouldn't stand out in a crowd. Why did they package so many women's bath products in milky-white containers?

Suddenly weary, he took the candles into the bedroom, put the mattress back on Gloria's bed, and cleared a space around it. In the course of this activity he discovered an old letter file, a flip-top cardboard box covered in green patterned paper, whose contents were on the floor. Letters, of course, and—*hmm*—two college yearbooks. Both Bryn Mawr, 1964 and 1938. Sure enough, one was Gloria's and the other belonged to her mother. The letters were from Agnes to Gloria, and from a friend named Ruth Warfel, a '38 classmate. She'd become Dean of Women at Bryn Mawr and appeared to be writing to Agnes about Gloria. Other letters from Agnes to Warfel. Family crises and fond recollections. Kelly realized he'd hit the jackpot, if only he could decipher it.

Then he thought about the bathroom window, which opened onto an alley behind the apartment. He took a candle into the bathroom and made sure the window was unlocked, and whether this way out of the building would be available if he needed it. He returned to the pile of letters, eager to read them more closely, and immediately fell asleep.

In his dream Kelly was heading downtown. Instead of wearing him out, the whole wild night had jolted him into preternatural alertness. The Wilson's pulsed through him like high-octane fuel. Even the sewer stink, now in full bloom, was a part of his power. The oncoming stream of pedestrians parted in front of him.

He reached Lloyd's apartment, his head on fire. Someone had jammed the downstairs door open with a newspaper. He went up the two flights and knocked.

"Who is it?" Helen's voice.

"Me. Kelly. Let me in."

"Kelly!" She opened the door, flashlight in hand. "What's that awful smell?"

He stepped inside. "The Mob tried to kill me tonight."

She stared at him for a second, disappeared into the darkness, came back with a bottle of rye. He took a long swig and immediately felt calmer, stronger.

"How's that."

"An improvement."

"Can you be moved?"

"Maybe. Why?"

"We've got to get you cleaned up. That smell is unbearable."

"Twenty-Four Hour Protection. Hey, better than Dial. They can't get close enough to shoot me."

"Come with me." She helped him to the bathroom. Looking around, it was clear the goons had tossed the place when they nabbed him. "There's a fresh towel on the rack. I'll see if I can find some of Lloyd's clothes for you."

When he came out she was cooking something by candlelight in the kitchen. "I hope you like hamburger."

He found two glasses and filled them with the whiskey, watching her from behind as she worked. She seemed smaller than usual, stooped or in some way compressed. Kelly looked more carefully. Yes, something was wrong.

Helen put a plate in front of him. "I couldn't see very well what I was doing. If you eat with your eyes closed, we'll be even."

"If I closed my eyes I couldn't keep them on you."

"Wow."

"I'm trying to win your confidence."

"Consider it done."

"I've told you about my adventure. Let's hear yours."

She tossed her head and tried to smile, but her lips made a tight line. Her eyes were brimming.

"Come on, Helen."

"It's just so—"

She began to cry, making an unpleasant, arduous sound. He stood behind her. Smoothing her hair, rubbing the tightness out of her neck. "Easy, baby."

"It's just been so shitty with Lloyd. I don't need to tell you what's going on with him." Then she told him. It took quite a while. His ankle began to ache, and he sat across from her again, poured them another round. She paused, sniffled. "I watched him change until the Lloyd I fell in love with didn't exist anymore. Now it's like I've lost him, even though he's still around."

The high cheekbones were what fascinated him. Half concealed by the fall of her hair, offset by the hurt pout of her lips, they made her seem violated yet intact. "You've been through a lot, Helen."

Suddenly they were standing. "I'm glad he's gone. I'm glad you're here." Her hands were on his hips, her head tilted back. Her lips parted. He could feel her breasts against his ribs. For an instant he was afraid. Then it was sadness. This was going to be their night, the finish of the old dream. They kissed. The sadness left. Kelly became anxious for the finish. Already he was thinking of finishing twice.

They took the bottle into the bedroom and found a nesting spot. They touched, spoke softly. Kelly began to unbutton her shirt. She arched her back. He untucked her shirttails and parted the material. She turned each breast to his touch. Her skin glowed in the candlelight, fragrant and soft. He could feel the heat it radiated against his cheek. That belly—so wide, enclosed by those long hips, its perfect bulge punctuated by the mysterious navel—disappeared discretely beneath the soft silk of her panties.

"Don't stop."

His balls ached.

She made noises, twisted beneath him like a cat. He slid the panties down and she kicked them off. The curve of her belly and the lines of her hips converged. He kissed and kissed that place where they came together. Her knees moved around his head, her hips surged at his touch. He was inside. Her flesh was all around him. She was the ocean. He was swimming in her promise.

Then, just as he began to come, he heard it. He recognized the tune the guy'd been whistling—it was the first few notes of "Tequila," over and over—d' *do* do do do d' *doohd* oo. His brains were the only part of him that made it through the window, splattered by Woody's bullet onto the lawn below.

Kelly woke screaming. The candles were guttered in their plates and the first hint of dawn leaked through the bedroom window. He got his breathing under control and went back in the bathroom to towel the sweat away. He saw, once again, that an exceedingly thin, porous membrane separated dreaming from reality. He understood how careful, how aware of the always-flowing currents he needed to be at all times. One silly little incident, helping a German tourist, say, or the intention to cuckold a friend, could, with no warning, knock him off course. Fatally. The thought lingered.

Eventually, strengthened by his musings, he buttoned his shirt, rolled up his sleeves, gathered the letter box and its contents, and took the D train to Bensonhurst.

Aunt Kay greeted him at her door, a loving smile creasing her aged features. "Kelly!" Then a momentary frown. "What's that awful smell?"

Junko Partner

The Mailman didn't even stop to pee. His mouth hurt from all the coke he'd gummed, and he swiped a 7UP from the cooler out front of the station in Connecticut where he gassed up. Leaving the engine running, he slapped a sawbuck in the sleepy attendant's paw and peeled out before the guy could even give him shit for not shutting his car down. He was totally jacked on Lloyd's speed, and even more cranked at the thought of—the *feel* of—the old Turk's load in the door panel beside his left elbow. His ticket, his future. No more bullshit schemes for him. From the first moment Kelly had popped that suitcase open on Lloyd's couch, he'd known exactly what he was going to do.

There were some nervous moments, however. Outside of Beverly, just half an hour from home, the car began to overheat, lost power, bucked, and coughed. He figured he'd blown a valve, maybe the head gasket, and his heart started hammering so hard, he thought he'd black out. He rolled the windows down, turned the heat on full to help the cooling system, and nursed it the rest of the way in the breakdown lane, letting it coast down hills in neutral. He didn't think he'd make it up the incline to his driveway on Webster

Street, but the old girl gave it everything she had, rolled to a stop, sighed, and erupted in billows of steam and burned-oil stench. He took the suitcase of Fitz Hugh Lanes from the backseat, locked the car up, and walked down to the Historical Society. It was seven a.m. The streets were his, just like the old days.

Soon the paintings were right back at the end of the bench, in their foam padding again, everything tidied up. He should have been exhausted—in fact, he did feel raggedy underneath—but he was just so damned glad to be in a mode where he was in control again. He savored that sensation, locking the building back up, standing on the sidewalk across from the Elks Club feeling the morning sun on his face, waving at Officer Randazza making his morning run down to Dulie's Dory for doughnuts.

He walked slowly past Mr. Manson Patillo's handsome Civil War–era house, inhabited now by his crazy great-great-granddaughter and her fifteen cats, down to Main, recalling that the post office had once dominated the corner of Main and Pleasant, before Brown's Department Store took over that key spot. It wasn't until the Depression that they built the new one, *his* post office, on Dale Avenue, as a public works project, Gloucester stonemasons doing all that lovely granite work. Those vaulting thirty-foot ceilings, like nobody knew enough to save space or heat in the Depression. Whenever Denny Mears crooned his doo-wop arriving, still drunk, for the morning shift, it echoed through the vast sorting room like he was singing in the shower.

Down eastward, the morning sun shone stronger now, where urban renewal was destroying the funky old waterfront in the name of bogus chamber of commerce visions of yacht slips and seafood restaurants. Past the head of the harbor and the Main Deck, remembering

June and the ump and all of it, just as if he'd straightened out and moved away and grown up and was coming back clean on a sparkling morning, walking the streets and recalling his youth. Up the Wall Street hill overlooking the harbor. Past Manny Perry's elephantine tenement—three floors of apartments at $125 a month, with a view of the harbor that you couldn't get in a millionaire's house, to the chicken coop of a dump on Amero Court, across from Perry's place. Up the rickety wooden fire escape, into Langer's fetid drug den to cop a set of works. Langer was curled in a sleeping bag under the front window.

"Langer. Langer." Toe in the ribs.

Finally the other man came around, his lips cracked and white, black stubble on his sunken cheeks. "Christ. You scared me."

The Mailman did his pantomime thing. Langer tumbled to it quickly, gathered up what was needed, and walked with him down Wall, over Eastern Avenue, up Webster, to his house. Papa Menezes was getting ready for his janitor's job at Gloucester Engineering, with Ilda there on the front porch waiting to see him off. She smiled and waved. Langer and the Mailman waved back.

All clear now. It was perfect. He'd take his cut in advance, just a little off the top of one of the bags out in the car. Have himself one last party before Lloyd arrived to sell the shit. Take his share of that and go to San Francisco. They had clinics there. Get clean, start his new life on the post office pension.

The old Turk's load tingled.

Langer tingled, too, waiting demurely while the Mailman disappeared, like it was some kind of goofy high school play. Of course he had the shit stashed in that wreck of a jalopy of his. Under a seat or in the glove compartment. He'd get high with the Mailman till it was gone, or drift off by himself if no more was forthcoming at the moment, then return late that night to check out the car, see if there was more. The Mailman would be pissed, but fuck him. He sure wasn't going to call the cops.

Presently the Mailman returned with a dentist's office Dixie cup half full of smack. Langer's eyes goggled. The guy had gotten into some bulk. Wow.

He took out his works, cooked up a spoonful, and fired a questioning look at his junko partner, the Mailman, who now seemed to have All the Time in the World. The voiceless one smiled and waved him on.

So Langer tied up, did himself, and jolted back when he let the rubber tubing loose. The rush came on as good as ever, but this time it did not stop. It crashed him through this sorry world and out—to where, he was amazed to realize, he truly wanted to be. This was the deal. This had been it all along. Just like going home. His eyes rolled to the top of his head, mouth went wide as the load climaxed. Then he stopped breathing and slumped off the chair, turned blue on the floor.

The Mailman realized pretty quickly what had happened. The shit was uncut. Langer had cooked it up like cheap street stuff and OD'd. The Mailman prodded him, slapped him, pushed on his chest to try to get the breathing started. Nothing doing. He dialed 911 and tried to explain the situation, but of course the dispatcher couldn't understand him. That didn't matter. The system would automatically give them his address.

He looked down at Langer. Hard. To fix the image in his mind for when he'd need it later. Then he went to the bank, cashed out the last of his savings, took a cab to Logan and a plane to San Francisco. They had clinics there.

Walking out on a fortune in heroin was easy. The Load was death to him now.

Of course it was too late by the time the cops responded to the Mailman's call. But Langer, off with Smoot and Richard Mundi, didn't mind. He looked compassionately down at his poor used-up body, fifteen feet below him now, with cops crawling over it like lobsters on a carcass at the bottom of the harbor. He was at peace, and peace was hard to come by, no matter what reality you inhabited.

True to the profile of the Mailman's life, no one realized he'd gone away until quite a while later. That was how he'd always wanted it, and in that respect he had greater success achieving his goals than most people do.

Helen and Lloyd

Helen returned from her Zen retreat in Vermont to find the apartment tossed and her husband passed out naked under a filthy towel, in the bathtub. He'd wet and shat himself, but the cleanup was pretty easy in the tub, and she was mellowed out from the retreat. By the time she'd straightened up the place Lloyd started to come around. She gave him two Miltowns and a glass of water. He looked at her for a long while, then thanked her.

That surprised her. He was very quiet, as he sat watching her clean, which surprised her more. Lloyd almost never shut up. She continued putting objects back in drawers and sweeping up broken glass and crockery, waiting for him to explain. He asked her if she wanted a cup of tea—things were getting *really* wiggy now.

"Helen ... I know this is a bummer." He hesitated, again uncharacteristically. "But I've ... I've b-been getting my mind around some heavy shit lately ... I want to go back to Massachusetts ... I want to get c-c-clean."

That was it. He'd finally bottomed out.

"I've just got a few—a few details to work out."

She looked at him, sighed. Same old bullshit. "I'm not sure I want to leave New York."

"No hassle."

She studied his face, trying to sort the crap from the reality. The bathtub scene had been kind of impressive. Maybe he really had hit bottom. But *a few details to work out*—how often had she heard that?

Helen looked and looked, but she just couldn't see to that bottom. She couldn't see what he truly wanted to do. Even worse, she couldn't see what she truly wanted to do. She'd been putting up with his antics for so long that she'd lost her bearings. She'd started out by falling in love with him, she knew that. But neither of them had ever wanted to take the hard way when it came to anything, so their relationship had just drifted along, with them having less and less in common. Leaving, though, seemed too much trouble. She'd been waiting for the inevitable end but was never resolved about it. Did she want the money or did she want Lloyd? Did she want him sick and gone, or healthy and here? She was as messed up as he, only not on drugs. The one immediate result of whatever Lloyd now wanted her to understand was that she was sick of his shit.

She rose from the table, grabbed the backpack she'd just carried down from Vermont, and said, "Fuck you, Lloyd," but quietly, under her breath.

Jarkey's Man

Just as Harry Jarkey was Kelly's man, Neil Genzlinger was Jarkey's man. He worked at the *Times* morgue and helped Jarkey do research for Kelly. But he also aspired to a writing career, and Jarkey was coaching him on getting his foot in the door. It was Genzlinger on the phone when Harry returned to his apartment on East Ninety-Fourth, hardly a thought in his head after two days with Irene. The ringing started when Harry was in the shower, and it kept up as he toweled off.

"Hey! I've been trying to reach you all afternoon."

"You reached me, pal."

"I went to see Kelly yesterday," Genzlinger told him. "He wasn't there, but his office was destroyed."

"Right. Well, there's been some stuff going on. Kind of difficult to explain."

"It doesn't look so good to me, Harry. About the office, I mean."

"I'll check it out and let you know." He put down the receiver.

Jarkey had to admit to some residual curiosity about Kelly's next move. Did he have the drugs? What was he going to do about the Mob? He dressed and walked down to Sammy's.

Norbert, nervously toweling glasses, gave him a queer look when he walked in.

"You seen Kelly?"

The bartender's color, Jarkey realized, wasn't so good. Not that tending bar had enhanced it. Finally Norbert leaned toward him and said miserably, "It was me. I gave him up."

"What are you talking about?"

"Three gorillas were waiting when I came into work the other day—right before the blackout. They were looking for Kelly. I told them to go down to Lloyd's. Couldn't think of any other way to get rid of them. I knew Kelly had a thing for Lloyd's wife, but I didn't figure he'd actually be there." He shook his head in self-disgust.

"And . . . ?"

"Helen called yesterday, asking if I'd seen him. Her place had been trashed, and Kelly's hat and gun were on the floor. I can imagine him forgetting his gun, but he'd never go anywhere without the hat."

"You don't know for sure they found him there."

"She talked to a neighbor who saw a guy nab him in front of the apartment and throw him in a car."

"Jesus."

Norbert, who hadn't touched a drop in thirty-three years, now squirted a few inches of ginger ale into a glass and tossed it back in a gulp. Jarkey had intended to share a consolatory drink, but the other man had aroused the memory of Kelly's last words—about how he had a surprise planned for the bad guys. He gave Norbert a reassuring pat on the shoulder and caught a cab down to the Lower East Side.

*   *   *

He found Lloyd sitting on the edge of the bed in his apartment—serene, contemplative, above it all—gazing back at earth across light-years of drug-induced brain damage. There was a pair of folded jeans in his lap and a small suitcase on the bed beside him. He'd probably been trying to get packed all day.

"Harry . . ."

"Lloyd, what happened to Kelly?"

"Oh." Flat, emotionless, like he'd just heard his dry cleaning was ready. Long pause. "They got him. When I was out. They got him and wrecked my place. They'll get you, too. But it doesn't matter. Because that stuff is going to get you all. It's evil . . ." His tone suddenly turned oracular. "I saw it last night." He paused. "I understand now."

What Jarkey understood was that Lloyd was in a state of shock—chemical or otherwise. "When did they toss your place, Lloyd? Were you here?"

"No. I was . . . out. Kelly was sleeping on the couch. But he was gone when I got back. Must've been when they nabbed him. Helen came but I sent her away. I didn't want her to get hurt. I'm waiting for them to come back."

"Waiting for them?"

"When they come I'm going to tell them where the heroin is, and they'll get it and it'll destroy them."

"That's a terrible idea, Lloyd. They'll kill you."

"You don't understand, Harry. It's more evil than they are. They'll think I'm doing them a favor."

"Evil, right." Jarkey was patient. "Where is it, Lloyd? You need to tell me, too."

"Yes." He unfolded the jeans, shook them out, folded them again, and put them back on his lap. "Kelly and I put the stuff in the door panel of the Mailman's car and he drove it to Gloucester. I used to live in Gloucester. I used to know the Mailman, too, except now he has a hole in his throat. We were going to go up there and help him fence it, like it came off the boats. Then I . . . changed my mind."

"I'm cool with that, Lloyd. But where is it? Where is it now?"

"Thirty-one Webster Street. Bottom of Portugee Hill. The Mailman lives in the basement apartment. I used to live on the top floor. The penthouse." He chuckled softly at some private recollection. "Get it if you want. It'll destroy you, too."

Lloyd was creeping him out. At that point Harry didn't care if the Newark heavies *did* come back and find him sitting there folding and refolding his pants. They'd storm in, Lloyd would tell them where the stuff was, and they'd kill him, just like Kelly. He could feel the menace gathering out there, like a very nasty storm. He needed shelter.

He called Irene, who told him to come back to her.

The Endless Summer

Maddy never said a word about the power failure the next morning—nobody in Wallis Sands cared much about what went on in New York—and Gloria didn't find out about it until that evening when she went down to Philbrick's to make her call. The headline on the pile of *Manchester Union Leaders* beside the brass cash register said, "Blackout Hits Northeast."

She asked Irene about it first thing.

"It was a weird night. But, Glo, I've got some bad news for you."

All Gloria could think of was the drugs. "Go ahead . . ."

"Your father had a heart attack at the airport. He's dead. Murchison and Kraft are taking care of things."

It shocked Gloria that all she felt at first was a kind of lightness. Then came the slam of something very complicated beneath the relief. "Give me a while, okay? I'll call you at your office later."

She wandered across the street to the tumble of boulders that marked the north end of the little sand beach. She sat looking over the water at the huge old hotels on the Isles of Shoals, illuminated like a floating metropolis by the westering sun. As if her mother and father were there now, in that mysterious Golden

City, and she could no more get to them than she could swim to Appledore Island.

The pain began to come on in waves, each stronger than the last. She wasn't going to be able to think her way through this, nor would her self-assurance help. Much as Kelly might've done, she worked through it, in her extremity, image by image. Oldest memories first—Daddy young and strong. She and Daddy playing. Daddy and Julie. Daddy coming home once when she was very young—she could absolutely hear his voice—and calling Mommy "Honey Bunch."

That one brought the tears; then wrenching sobs gutted up from a place she'd never been before. The images slid into patterns. She gasped for breath, and slowly the racking waves diminished. She remembered her mother's hugs, and the way Daddy's pride in her—his and Mommy's both—had felt warm like the sun in summer.

As that part of their lives expanded for her, all the troubled present shrank down to its rightful trifling size. Then she understood it was going to be very difficult for a while, but that it had been essentially right with Daddy and her, as it had been with Mommy, and for exactly this reason she would be okay. Missing him would hurt, but she'd be able to function. She thanked the both of them, her parents, for everything they'd given her, wished them peace, and stared over the ocean as the island beyond turned red, then gray. Eventually she made her shaky way down the road to Maddy's.

It was an impressive job of self-persuasion, and whenever she thought of it afterward she knew she'd only been able to pull it off because of Maddy and that womb of a place on the marsh by the edge of the sea. She'd been damned lucky to land there.

The Jar

Lloyd sat on the edge of his bed for a few hours after Harry left, a second at a time. While he was sitting, he thought about his situation. The Mafia guys kept not showing up, but his encounter with Jarkey had given him an idea. If they didn't come, the thing to do was call them. Eventually, even in his hinky state, the thought gained purchase and Lloyd shuffled from his bed into the big front room, found the phone, lifted the receiver from its cradle, got a dial tone, called a guy he knew who knew a guy in the Newark gang, and got word to them that way. It was an impressive sequence for a man with his synaptic challenges.

In high gear now, Lloyd phoned Kevin Gallagher. He wanted the Communists in on this, too. But Gallagher, thoroughly tamed by his hours in the closet, didn't bother with the *foco*. He reported Lloyd's news directly to Spaulding.

Lloyd considered calling the cops for an encore, but decided that'd be overdoing it. The cops, it turned out, were *good*, that is, against the drugs. He didn't want them getting hurt.

Dead Kelly

Jarkey was beside himself. "Kelly's dead, Irene. The mob guys grabbed him at Lloyd's. One of Helen's neighbors saw the whole thing go down. It had to be a rubout. He didn't even take his hat."

He paced her office floor, working the rosary of his doubts and fears. Would Irene be safe now or were they still out there, hunting people down? Was he in danger? What about Gloria? And what would he do without Kelly? Without the paycheck? The wacky jobs?

She took him to a sandwich place, and eventually he calmed down. Jarkey filled her in about the Mailman and the drugs and Gloucester. She questioned him closely, lawyerlike, but it was hard for him to concentrate because the hurt had started leaking in. His mind teemed with random recollections—the unique smell of Kelly's aftershave and whiskey breath, the time he'd actually crouched down behind the outraged husband and Kelly had pushed the guy over and they'd both run like naughty schoolboys. There had been a kind of innocence to it all. Even in the worst of their snooping and petty deceptions, Kelly's strange simplicity imposed a freshness, an element of adventure, a sense of high purpose.

Irene told him he'd be safer if he stayed with her for a while.

He assented, since nothing would make him happier. However, he explained that, first, he needed to be alone with his thoughts for a while. She told him to be careful.

He headed south across the city, toward Kelly's office, striding into the huge ache of the detective's death, wondering at how weird it was that Irene had come into his life just as Kelly had left it.

That was when the guilt hit him. He'd been so smitten with Gloria and Irene that he'd forgotten about Mundi. Gloria's dad had set his friend up. He lashed himself for a block or two. He should have warned him.

But he and Gloria *had* warned Kelly. Was there anything he could have done differently? Traded two days of bliss with Irene for—what? Tagged along after Kelly, trying to protect him, getting himself killed, too, in the process? Why was love always so complicated? Why did it have to hurt so much?

He wrestled with ugly imaginings of Kelly's last moments. It seemed weirdest that there was no one to tell. No partner, no significant other, no family. Irene and Gloria, of course, but they had no real sense of who Kelly had been. Pepsi? Kelly had *paid* her, for crying out loud. Even the detective's so-called friends were nothing more than business associates or, hell—tell it like it is—stoolies. It wasn't until he approached the neon sign over Sammy's Undersea Lounge that he remembered Norbert.

Sammy's was closed.

Good Old Julie, Again

Gloria had her shit together for her next phone call to Irene. All business now, she received the news about Lloyd, the Mailman, and Kelly in a surprisingly philosophical manner.

"I knew he was stupid, but I figured he'd be shifty enough not to get caught. Did Harry find out what happened?"

"Apparently Kelly got nabbed in Lloyd's apartment. Of course the drugs were long gone by that time."

"Too bad about him, but good news for us. Plus, it settles the problem of Harry betraying his boss."

"Truly."

"And the stuff's in Massachusetts?"

"Lloyd's hometown, according to Harry. A fishing port."

Gloria paused, thinking some more. "Well, it is what it is. Kelly's gone and Lloyd's brain-dead. The stuff is there for the taking. Either DiNoto knows what's up, or he doesn't. If he doesn't, chances are he will soon. We'll just have to get there first."

"I still don't like it."

"Irene, stop doing that! You're already in, and you know it." Gloria was surprised to hear herself talking this way. But it was just the nudge her friend needed.

"Okay, okay."

The load's gravity enveloped them.

"We've got to get some muscle. I'll call Julie Roth and try to get him in on this. After what happened to Daddy and Mossman, he might be interested in laying some hurt on Mr. D. If he leaves the city tonight, we can meet in Gloucester early tomorrow morning. We'll roust this guy when he's getting up for work. Whatever it is he does. He's a mailman?"

"It's a little confused. I think he's a laryngectomee."

"A what?"

"Throat cancer . . . Gloria, I just want you to know. I'm going to bring Harry."

"He's not exactly muscle, but he's got his uses." Not a twinge of jealousy. She was clean as a whistle.

Despite her confident tone, Gloria knew her call to Julius Roth would be difficult. She was having trouble thinking of a sure-fire way to persuade him that further outraging the Mafia would be the thing to do. So she decided to plead for help, banking on the affection that had existed between them all her life. His reply left her gasping into the receiver.

"I'm in," he said.

"In?"

"Your father's out, sweetie. He always wanted you to take over the company, and I'm about all that's left of the company."

"I thought you said there was no company."

"Depends on how you look at it. Creditors are lined up six deep, and Mundi Enterprises is headed for bankruptcy court. If there's anything left after DiNoto's guys pick it apart. But what if there was a new Mundi Enterprises? A left-wing legal aid provider? We know how to put a company together, and it seems we have competent legal advice."

"Julie, are you serious?"

"I was getting burned out in Newark. Waxing that kid from the projects was the last straw."

"In with Irene? The movement? Everything?"

"The thought of cracking heads for a just cause inspires me."

"Jesus."

Officers Wolf and Sponagle

For years the Gloucester cops had been holding steady at 30 percent rotten, which was probably about the national average. It was a cultural thing on the force. Rookies of a certain persuasion would be drawn into the society of their bent elders, quickly turning bent themselves. The good cops put up with their foul nestlings because to do otherwise would damage the appearance of solidarity upon which their civic franchise depended. There were no bad politicians in Gloucester—or, they were all bad—but they tended to run either weak or strong. The weak ones worked with the bad cops. The strong pretended the bad cops didn't exist because they didn't want to have their kids busted on prom night, or wind up in the slammer themselves for a DWI whether they were drunk or not, or wake up to four flat tires, or have the wife get scary phone calls. Nobody wanted any part of that.

As it happened, two of that 30 percent were on duty when the 911 came in about the junkie on Webster Street. Officers Wolf and Sponagle responded to the call and recognized Langer. Either he'd OD'd or someone had slipped him a hotshot. They put Langer's works in an evidence bag, and a little of the smack into another one, for lab tests. They secured the scene, searched the premises, conducted interviews. Made their notes. They retained the rest of the Mailman's Dixie cup for personal use. Then, after the ambulance hauled the corpse off, they paid a visit to the offices of the Continental Insurance Agency to check in with Mr. Reardon.

"A fucking Dixie cup?"

"There's definitely something strange going on, Mr. Reardon. The guy was OD'd, meaning it was either bad shit or uncut. And look at this." Wolf produced the Dixie cup. "Who scores smack in paper cups? It's like he scooped it out of a barrel."

"You guys search the place?"

"Clean as a whistle. But you gotta think there's something out there somewhere."

"Very interesting, boys." Reardon turned things over in his mind. He knew the building. His slumlord cousin had owned it briefly, then sold it to a hardworking Portugee immigrant who lived there. Come to think of it, that was where the Mailman slept, down in his cave at the bottom. Reardon recalled his recent interview with the poor bastard, and thought for the second time in ages about the Mailman's former neighbor, Lloyd Chamberlain, turning his crummy drug deals down in Manhattan. Very interesting, indeed.

He looked across his desk at the two cops.

"Why the fuck are you still here?"

There was an awkward silence. Then Reardon remembered the Dixie cup and pushed it back across to Officer Wolf. Sponagle gave him a shit-eating grin.

When Mr. DiNoto called that night to inform Reardon that a shipment of goods had possibly found its way to Gloucester, Reardon had plenty to tell him. DiNoto said he was sending some people up and would appreciate it if Reardon made sure that everyone stayed the fuck out of their way.

Reardon, acutely aware of his place in the scheme of things, told Mr. D. he'd take care of that detail. DiNoto said, "You bet you will," and hung up.

By the time Agent Spaulding called the Gloucester cops, Wolf and Sponagle were out snorting their smack with a couple of part-time hookers. The desk man on duty gave him Chief Movalli's home number, and Movalli, who'd read Wolf's report, was able to inform Spaulding that only a small quantity of heroin had been found at the scene.

Spaulding told Movalli to stand by, that he and another agent would be in Gloucester next morning to assess the situation themselves. Movalli, who was not one of the bad cops, realized Wolf and Sponagle would be back on duty and nearly had a bird. He suggested that Spaulding meet him at his office first for a briefing. Spaulding assented, but told Movalli there were security issues involved, as well as possible interstate felonies, so the FBI would be handling this themselves. No way the locals were going to horn in on his bust.

Rosy

Very early next morning Gloria left a note for Maddy that read, *I feel so much better now. Thank you for being a friend.* She had three days' credit on her bill; if she ever needed to come back, Maddy would remember her fondly.

She retraced her drive to Route 1, down the New Hampshire Turnpike and Route 95, then up Route 128 toward Gloucester. The Starship sliced through time and space of its own volition, leaving Gloria free to think about Wallis Sands. It really had been like landing on another world, she decided, where something in the atmosphere changed her, like in that old stoner flick *Forbidden Planet*—though just the opposite.

A sign at Route 133 promised Gloucester. She turned off the highway and wound through marshlands and granite clumps fronting patches of woods, with New England cottages and turn-of-the-century Queen Anne–style houses tucked into hills. Then, in the midst of her reverie, the road came to a T and the vast harbor spread out before her, glinting gold and blue in the early morning light. Far out over the water a line of trawlers headed seaward, and gulls wheeled above them like a cloud of gnats.

She turned left at the harbor, toward town, past Pavilion Beach, where the Mailman had once taken his midday swims, coming to a stop where the harbor front road intersected with Main and Rogers at a gas station called Tally's. She pulled up to one of the six pumps under the canopy and a blimp of a man waddled out of the office. He had a matted gray crew cut and wore a dirty gas station jumpsuit that said ROSY over the breast pocket, which was angled forty-five degrees from vertical by the man's immense belly. He smiled warmly at Gloria. No teeth.

"Fill 'er up, please. High-test. And I need some help with directions."

"Sure thing," he wheezed. "Just let me get the pump started."

He came around to her door and she told him the address. He nodded, went back to his office, and consulted a phone book. "The Portugee Club is 27-29 Webster Street. A big brown building about a quarter mile up the hill on the right. So number thirty-one would be right next door. Just go down around the corner here— that's Rogers. Then a half mile or so and left on Eastern at a place called the Main Deck. Then your one . . . two . . . *third* left would be Webster. Can't miss it."

Thus Rosy recapitulated the route of the Mailman's weekly pub crawls, and unwittingly memorialized his Last Mile Walk with Langer.

Gloria paid up and, as she thanked him, regarded his bulk with a clinical eye, wondering how they could possibly have found a grease monkey suit that big.

True to his word, Gloria did not miss it—a ramshackle triple-decker with green asphalt shingles. She did a drive-by and was pleased to see a '56 Buick out front. Certainly old enough to be

- 3-

the Mailman's car, described by Lloyd only as a "junker." The stuff could still be in the door panel, maybe in the house. They'd have to make sure he didn't run, calm him down, convince him to play along. Probably they'd wind up taking him back to New York to work out a deal. She'd have Harry drive with her and the Mailman and Julie could take the stash.

There didn't seem to be any activity in the basement apartment or anywhere else in the building, but it was early. She parked in the lot at the Portuguese-American Club and waited for her friends, breathing deeply, trying to recall the calm that had been hers only a while ago.

It was forty long minutes before Roth's Olds slid in next to her. Gloria motioned them over. Irene and Harry got in the backseat, each carrying a coffee. Roth sat in front. He seemed placid. Jarkey looked grim, as if he expected the worst. Irene, however, looked even grimmer.

She and Gloria commenced a round of nervous small talk.

"Ladies," said Roth. "Either of you have any idea what's going to go down here?"

"Right." Gloria gave an uncertain grin. "Sitting here for an hour hoping I didn't have to tackle this Mailman guy myself, I've gotten some thinking done. Harry, how bad was Lloyd?"

"Mentally? Physically?"

"Everything."

"When I saw him yesterday, he was definitely on the edge of psychosis. For him the deal with the smack has shifted into some kind of cosmic morality play. On top of that, he's got this thing about telling the Mafia where the stuff is so they'll get destroyed along with us."

"So he tells them, but then they kill him?"

"Or he winds up in Bellevue."

"Either way," Roth broke in, "he's out of the picture. Right?"

He addressed Jarkey directly, making as if he were the expert. Consequently, Jarkey got more comfortable, which was how Roth needed him. "Yeah. Kelly's dead and Lloyd's a basket case."

"So I guess we're the Mailman's new partners."

"I like that," said Gloria. "What are the odds he'll buy it?"

A moment of silence, then Roth spoke again. "You want to talk about odds? What are the odds that Lloyd really did get through to DiNoto, and his boys have already been here? Or that they're inside right now tearing out wallboard? Or that they'll be here in five minutes?"

"Ten to one against," ventured Jarkey.

Gloria shook her head. "They don't know Lloyd from a hole in the wall. Do you seriously think they'd go charging across three states because some crack-brained tipster tells them the Apocalypse is waiting for them in Gloucester, Mass.?"

Roth opened his door. "This is still time-critical, kids. Let's get it done."

In fact, that was exactly what the Mafia did—they went charging across three states on the advice of some crack-brained tipster, reinforced, of course, by solid information from Reardon. Luckily for Gloria and her friends, the Street Brothers had a little trouble getting organized.

Lloyd had called Doc Viera in Newark and told him the deal was too big, too dangerous. He'd realized he was in way over his head. He was ratting out Kelly and the Mailman and he didn't want any reward, just to be left alone. He wanted to get cleaned up. He made his case to Doc Viera with a druggie's cunning and Viera bought it. He told Mr. D., and Mr. D. called Woody, for whom the light clicked on immediately.

"Oh, fuck. That musta been the loser with the apartment where we got Kelly. I tossed the place, but there was nothing to connect him with the French stuff. I thought Kelly had just been hiding there. He was some kinda pusher—street-level shit—but no way did I connect him with our stuff. Sorry, Mr. D."

The only qualities Mr. D. required of his men were honesty, loyalty, and some small measure of competence. He had learned not to expect people to perform beyond their capabilities. "That's okay, Woody. I'll call Reardon and get the particulars. Then I want the three of you to beat it up there as fast as you can. Don't take any shit. Don't buy any stories. Don't come back without the goods."

It was past midnight by this time. Vince, unfamiliar with East Coast highways, went straight up I-95 to Maine instead of turning off at 128. They didn't realize their mistake until Kittery—when Woody suddenly remembered Maine was north of Massachusetts. So that put them a little behind schedule. The funny thing was, driving up 95 that dawn, they'd passed the Starship headed down to Gloucester at warp speed.

Portugee Hill

There were two windows, right at ground level, looking down into the Mailman's dugout apartment. No lights were on, but they could see the room was a disaster. The Mailman's entry door had a shed built around it. This contained a fifty-gallon kerosene drum, a pair of boots, foul-weather gear, and rusted gardening tools. It smelled of cat spray. Roth, in the lead, nodded approvingly. If there were a scene at the door, at least they'd have a little privacy.

Taking the snub-nosed S&W from his jacket pocket, he tucked it into his belt. Jarkey edged up beside him and peered through the glass at the top of the door. The kitchen was similarly dark and empty. "Maybe they've already been here," he whispered. "It's a mess."

"Let's find out," said Roth, and pounded on the door. The wall rattled, but there was no response.

The shed began to fill with jangled, disparate vibes. Gloria knew this was the moment on which everything turned. It was her play, her chance to prove herself to Irene, certainly, but also to Julie who, amazingly, was supporting her. Or maybe he had been all along. Irene understood that it was Gloria's show and was content to have it so. But she was at war with herself. Why was she here? What if something went wrong and they got caught with drugs? She wouldn't be much help then, would she? But what if things went the way Gloria wanted and they wound up with hundreds of thousands of dollars in the fund? Money from selling poison that would kill hundreds of people. Destroy countless families. Could she live with that? If the heroin ruined more lives than she might save, where was the gain? She felt sick. To Jarkey it all seemed unreal, like a movie of the four of them. How could there be no Kelly? How could there be Irene? How could he be standing on the other side of the door from millions of dollars' worth of heroin? Roth was playing out in his head possible sequences of what might come next. But catching the whiff of nervous perspiration in the air of the entry shed, he realized his troops were on the edge of losing it.

He motioned Jarkey back and got ready to put his shoulder to the door. Harry edged toward the shed's opening, forcing the two women outside. Gloria turned back toward the street and saw a little girl standing there, watching. She might've been eight, with long raven hair, olive skin, and luminous black eyes. She showed no sign of shyness or fear. As if she'd been expecting them.

Gloria gave the girl a warm smile and a gentle "Hello." This kid would need to be dealt with. "My name's Gloria. What's yours?"

"Ilda."

"We're friends. From out of town. We came to visit."

"He's gone."

"Gone?"

"Yes, he left. Wait. I'll show you." She disappeared around the front corner of the house.

The mood shifted instantly. Gloria said it for the four of them. "The fuckers beat us here."

Roth nudged his bulk against the door and it popped open. The kitchen was dominated by a cast-iron kerosene stove. All the drawers in the other room had been emptied, bed pulled apart. There weren't many places to hide ten kilos of heroin. Roth examined them all.

The little girl came back with her papa's copy of the *Gloucester Daily Times*. Just below the fold on the front page the headline read, "Local Man Found Dead." His name was Martin Langer and he was forty-two. The cause had been a probable drug overdose. Police had been summoned to the 31 Webster Street apartment by an anonymous call. Foul play was not suspected. Traces of a class D substance were found at the scene. Pending an autopsy, scheduled for later in the week, no further details were available.

"Papa said they were bad men. But I liked the Mailman. I taught him how to talk after his operation."

It had to be the pull of the old Turk's load, dragging them off course. Ilda was telling them, plain as day, what had happened. But they, for all their intelligence, were not understanding what she was saying.

"Must have sampled some of the product," Roth told them. "And OD'd." He was remembering Smoot, back in Newark, and Kelly dead in some Mafia hideout. Now the Mailman.

Irene rode the edge of Roth's thinking. She felt tragedies and deaths, then a rush of mortal sadness. She bit her lower lip and stared out the window. Jarkey gazed at her anxiously, beaming her a psychic Get Well card. She refused it.

Gloria pushed ahead. "Honey, did anyone else come here after ... you know?"

Ilda saw immediately that these grown-ups had misunderstood her, that they thought Langer was the Mailman, and she wanted to correct their mistake. But she could feel how nervous they were. The lady seemed nice, but maybe they weren't the Mailman's friends.

"Just the police."

"Did you talk to them?"

"No. They were mean to Mama because she doesn't speak English." The little girl seemed so gorgeous and calm, in the midst of their squalid angst and nasty business, that she might have been an apparition.

Gloria shot Roth a look. "Think the cops nabbed it?"

"Then they would've written it up as a drug bust," Roth told her.

"Not if they stole it."

"It's a lot of dope. They'd have to be *really* crooked," he said, pursing his lips.

They paused for a moment, pondering how really crooked the Gloucester cops might be. Then Gloria resumed her interrogation.

"The police came, honey, and they looked all around, right?"

"Yes."

"Did anyone else come here after the police left?"

"Mr. Schultz came, and his friend, the woman."

"Mr. Schultz?"

"He was the Mailman's friend. After the police left, he came and took the car away."

The car! "You mean, that one out front doesn't belong to the Mailman?"

"That's Herbie's. On the third floor."

"Ilda, we need to find the Mailman's car."

Ilda wanted these people to go away now. There was definitely something wrong with them, and they were not the Mailman's friends. She said, "Wait. I'll ask Mama."

They followed her around to the front steps, to the apartment above the Mailman's. Ilda went in and reappeared with a heavyset woman in a print dress. Ilda asked her something in Portuguese and the woman gave a lengthy reply.

"After the policemen left, the Mailman's car was blocking Papa in and he had to go to work. So he called Mr. Schultz, and Mr. Schultz came and towed it away."

"Where does Mr. Schultz live, honey?"

She asked her mother, who shrugged. "She doesn't know," Ilda reported.

They walked back to the parking lot of the Portuguese-American Club and noted the sign posting its dire warning that unauthorized vehicles would be towed at the owner's expense. This didn't seem likely, but there was no point being sloppy. Roth parked down the street and the four of them got back into Gloria's car.

Gloria told them, "Maybe Rosy can help us."

"Rosy?'

"Wait till you meet him."

The Kaminsky Brothers

They found a Gloucester phone book in a booth on the way back to Tally's. To their relief, only one Schultz was listed. Rosy directed them to Church Street, the site of the Mailman's first long-term relationship and, probably, his happiest days. Faye and Schultzie's house was a cramped brown two-story, squeezed in among a row of similarly cramped houses across from the Unitarian church.

Gloria and Irene stayed in the car this time, so that Roth and Jarkey could do the hard, slightly menacing approach. Private eyes or insurance investigators. Faye was completely unimpressed.

"Friends of the Mailman's? That's a good one. He owe you money?" She led them to the kitchen table where she and Schultzie were smoking cigarettes and drinking coffee from thick mugs. Schultzie was skinny, about one hundred fifty pounds, and dressed in tidy khaki work clothes. He smelled of Wildroot Cream Oil.

"Actually, ma'am, we're looking for his car."

"*His* car?" erupted Schultzie. "That's rich. I loaned it to him for a weekend three years ago and I never got it back. Never saw a nickel either."

"Aww, lighten up," Faye told him. "Poor guy."

"Yeah, well. Anyway, the guy upstairs, Menezes, he calls me and says the Mailman's car is blocking him in. And the Mailman's gone. So I go over, and of course the place is locked up, and the car is, too, but I still have my other set of keys. Wouldn't you know, she won't start. So I pop the hood, and he's blown the seal, cracked the block. Trashed it. So I call Kaminsky's and they tow it away."

Roth got directions, then he and his companions sped off to Kaminsky's, a smallish junkyard at the end of a railroad spur in the industrial part of town. On one side of the yard was a tar-paper shack with a hand-lettered OFFICE sign atop the door. The four of them, hot for the load, spilled into the room like Keystone Kops.

There, uniformly squat and burly, were Joe, Benny, and Rem Kaminsky, enjoying their mid-morning coffee and doughnuts—the three of them balding exactly the same way. Same faces, schnozzes, smiles, each bearing the same uncanny resemblance to beloved Red Sox center fielder Dom DiMaggio, the L'il Perfessor, brother of Joe. (DiMaggio, not Kaminsky.) Joe Kaminsky and Benny were on stools at the counter up front, Rem at the desk in back.

Rem spoke first. "The Mailman's Ford? Sure. Bought it from Schultzie for ten bucks. Stripped the starter, the generator, and the radiator, but that was it. The thing was a wreck. Too many Ford parts around anyhow. No market for 'em."

"We just need to look at it. We might want to buy it back."

"Look at it? Sure. Benny, show them where it is."

Benny walked around from behind the counter, opened the door, and pointed into the yard.

They stared, searched, squinted hard for their heroin. Harry looked at Irene. Irene looked at Gloria. Gloria looked at Julie, who willed the mound of scrap metal to resolve itself into a heap of crushed automobiles—not squeezed into bricks, but pancaked, obviously, by the Kaminskys' homemade car squasher, a huge hydraulic rig in a frame of I beams. A crane with a giant magnet stood poised over the pile just as the Kaminskys had left it when they retired to their office for coffee. Off to the side of the crane were two railroad cars on which the squashed autos were being loaded. The front car was already full.

"There it is," said Benny. "On one of them freight cars. Prob'ly near the bottom of the first one, since it came in last."

Rem pitched in from behind them. "We ain't that big here. Can't have these clunkers hanging around. We were scheduled to get a load picked up today, so we crunched it right away. Otherwise it'd be parked right there where you're standing. Bad timing, I guess."

The Bigger Picture

In the bigger picture, contrary to Rem Kaminsky's assessment, their timing had actually been pretty good. As the four dejected opportunists slunk out of Gloucester, Vince, Woody, and the Mushroom arrived on the scene. They deconstructed the Mailman's apartment, then took the Buick apart right on the street.

Wolf and Sponagle had just come on duty, still high from their evening with the girls. Wolf got the neighbor's complaint call from the dispatcher and told Sponagle, "Oh, fuck. It's the car."

"What's the car?"

"That junker that Kaminsky towed away after Langer croaked. That's what all this is about. We got so wrapped up with the stiff, we never thought about where the Dixie cup came from. Five'll get you ten that fucking car had been the transport. Now a crew of Mob guys is over there tearing up someone else's car." Not feeling as good as they had prior to the complaint call, they drove to Webster Street.

What they found there was Vince slashing away at the backseat of the Buick with a buck knife. Woody's big black Lincoln was parked just behind. He was standing with his arms crossed over his chest, watching the approach of the cruiser.

Sponagle rolled his window down. "'Scuse me, fellahs. I think the vehicle you're looking for has been towed to Kaminsky's."

Woody looked disdainfully at him. Then he noted that Wolf had activated neither siren nor lights. The fuckers were bent. "Where did you say?"

"Kaminsky's junkyard. If you'd like, you can follow us."

Vince had stopped slashing. Vince and Woody looked at the cops, then at one another. The Mushroom was looking at a bird in the little apple tree across the way.

"Why not?"

Wolf radioed in that the situation on Webster Street had been resolved. Unfortunately, Chief Movalli, who'd just finished briefing Agents Spaulding and Voorhees, intercepted the call.

"What the fuck is going on over there?" He had a pretty good idea what the fuck, in fact. He ached for the chance to get Wolfie and his lard-ass partner to incriminate themselves, hoping against hope one of them would let something slip. Spaulding was standing right beside him, monitoring every word.

But Wolf wouldn't bite. He resolved to let Movalli handle the situation. The son of a bitch could go ahead and deal with Mr. Reardon. End of Movalli.

"Appears to be a case of mistaken identity, Chief, involving a motor vehicle that was towed to Kaminsky's after that 911."

"Get back to the station, Wolf."

"Yes sir."

Chief Movalli hustled Spaulding and Voorhees into his cruiser and screamed over to Kaminsky's. Agent Spaulding told Movalli to pull into a driveway at the end of Cleveland Street and he and

Voorhees proceeded into the yard on foot. Spaulding wanted this one bad. He could hear the load moaning.

Wolf and Sponagle arrived a minute or two later. Sponagle spotted the back of the chief's black-and-white in the driveway and waved his finger wildly at it. Wolf pulled over and motioned the Mob guys to stop.

They did not stop. The Lincoln accelerated around Wolf's cruiser, down the length of Cleveland Street, and pulled up inside the gates of Kaminsky's junkyard.

Spaulding and Voorhees, making a preliminary inspection of the yard prior to interrogating the owners, recognized the abrupt arrival of a Lincoln with New Jersey plates as a potential threat. Spaulding was standing on the driver's side of the car, about twenty feet in front. Voorhees was the same distance off the passenger's side. Both men drew their weapons.

Vince and Woody, sitting in the front seat behind tinted windows, recognized these Feds from the Tishman Building. Woody had been making lists, uncharacteristically, of the people he'd wasted, and the places in which he'd wasted them. Vince had been scrupulously not-thinking about wasting more people. They were cranked up as it was, and residually annoyed that they'd even *had* to get cranked up to go on this nightlong goose chase. The sight of the agents pitched them into a gorgeous rage.

Vince said, "Oh, you fucking cunts."

The Lincoln's front doors flew open and the Street Brothers blazed away. Point Blank. Bonnie and Clyde, baby. Spaulding and Voorhees jerked, screamed, crumbled.

Mad for blood and heroin now, the Street Brothers stalked to the office to finish their job.

The Kaminsky brothers, having heard the commotion outside, were more than ready. Vince and Woody burst through the door, and Joe and Bennie cut them in half with matching 12-gauge sawed-off shotguns. There'd been trouble in the junkyard before, and the Kaminskys weren't about to take any shit from anyone, a fact neither Mr. D. nor Vince nor Woody could have been expected to know. The plywood front wall blasted through into the yard, splattered with gore. The blood of Woody and Vince commingled in what was left of the doorway. Together at last.

The Mushroom sensed trouble and went to investigate. Rem had one for him, too.

It rained heavily later that day, which helped a little with the blood in the yard. The remainder of the old Turk's load went into solution and leaked through the bottom of the first flatcar onto the tracks, where it eventually biodegraded, then disappeared.

Plus Four

Over in Bensonhurst, Kelly painted Aunt Kay's kitchen. Things had to be moved from each wall, then the surface behind had to be scrubbed of the decades of grease and dust and nicotine deposited by Uncle Frank (eight years deceased) and his damned cigarettes. It was a slow process, but that was how they both wanted it.

The painting had been Kelly's idea. He needed to stay for a spell and wanted to make himself useful. Aunt Kay was all in favor but insisted on buying the paint. She got Spread Satin, which someone had told her didn't smell. Once Kelly began spreading it, they joked about how it stank. The color reminded him of faded bananas. She loved it. She didn't ask why he was there, what had caused his unannounced arrival, or how long he'd stay. He loved her for that.

She lived alone now, but her old friend Rita the hairdresser lived right in the building, so if she needed help, a ride to the doctor or whatever, Rita was there. Bustling about the place, Aunt Kay seemed hale, pink, self-sufficient.

While he cleaned and painted, they talked. They talked about the part-time job Rita had once gotten for her, applying makeup to the corpses at McGuire's Funeral Home, and how Rita had gotten a friend to pretend to be a stiff. Kay had gone in to work on her and she'd sat up. They talked about the Yanks who were in the midst of a terrible season, salvaged only by the fact that the Mick had already hit his five hundredth dinger. They talked about his mother, Aunt Kay's sister, and the old days. What was it that had made Kay and Kelly's mom laugh so much when they were together? Just like little girls. She reminded him about the time they'd borrowed a car and gone upstate (anywhere north of Yonkers was "upstate," and they'd barely made it out of Yonkers) and had a picnic, and Kelly had been stung by that nest of yellow jackets, and Uncle Frank had rescued and soothed him. Uncle Frank had been a cop, too good and too simple to rise in the system, and had retired, a saint on his beat. The line at his wake stretched three blocks.

They talked about him through the cleaning and painting of the wall behind the stove, how he'd loved *The Honeymooners*, especially Ralph Kramden, and how odd that was because he was not at all like the blustering Jackie Gleason character. They talked and talked.

Kelly was reminded of a story he'd heard on the radio once. It had been about how POWs during the Korean War would sit around in the prison camp and together remember a movie they'd seen. Each soldier would contribute some bit about the movie, and the more the bits came together, the more other bits were remembered, until they could put the whole movie back together. That's what it felt like talking with Aunt Kay. Though never a word was said about Kelly's father, Irish Johnny, who'd ruined the life of Aunt Kay's sister and driven her to an early death.

After dinner Kelly would take a long walk on Nineteenth Avenue, during which he'd smoke his nightly couple of cigarettes. At

Milestone Park he'd do his push-ups and sit-ups, and chin himself on the jungle gym. Then he'd go home and watch the ball game or Lawrence Welk with his aunt, sipping daintily from his nightly half-pint of Wilson "That's All" blended whiskey, still wrapped in its paper bag. Beside him Kay worked her bottomless decanter of sherry, kept behind the magazine rack. Later, Kelly would stretch out on his bed and study the letters from Gloria's apartment. It was still a challenge to get to the bottom of the story they told. They were disturbing, that was the problem. But murky. Mostly they seemed to talk about Agnes's career, though he thought he could detect a looming threat, a sense of menace. Why wasn't her husband protecting her? Was someone stalking her? Kelly couldn't figure it out.

Bedtime came early at Aunt Kay's. For Kelly the regular hours, healthy exercise, and diminished whiskey intake felt like Olympic training. For Aunt Kay it was simply a good moment. She was wise enough to understand the fragility of life, and she made sure to take joy in it, and in him.

After the kitchen was done, he painted the outside hallway and the stairs going down. They both knew this marked the end of their time together. Kelly could feel the Problem out there, and when the wave gathered under him once again, he rode off with it.

"Irene Kornecki's office."

"Is this Irene?"

"Who shall I say is calling?"

"Kelly."

"Kelly's dead."

"Let's keep it that way for now. I need to find Julius Roth. I need to talk to him."

"About what?"

"I think you know about what. We've got a situation that needs getting taken care of."

"I see." It had to be Kelly. But where had he been—and what had happened to him?

She knew some stuff. Like the way DiNoto had gone nuts after the loss of the Street Brothers and his heroin. The rumor was he'd taken out a couple of cops in Gloucester. It was definitely a fact that he'd whacked Murchison and Kraft, the only two attendees at Mundi's burial—other than the priest—right in the cemetery. Then Gallagher, on the street in broad daylight, execution-style. The priest had taken a leave of absence. Jarkey was staying with relatives in Illinois. Gloria had moved in with Maddy, and Roth was ... well, only Gloria knew where. The city, for some, was frozen in a reign of terror, with DiNoto's soldiers lurking everywhere.

Now Kelly had shown up. Gloria and Harry had offered seriously conflicting appraisals of him. Irene had no idea what his capabilities actually were, but he had apparently survived being dead. Perhaps he could help.

Roth and Kelly met a few weeks later at a diner in Newark. They put Roth's car in a lot and Kelly drove him in the black Fairlane past DiNoto's office, then west on the turnpike to Pottersville. He stopped at a stone drive in a thickly wooded area.

"There's a gate about fifty yards in," Kelly told him. "Armed gatekeeper. The driveway goes uphill another quarter mile beyond that. The whole lot is clean as a pool table, and the house is on top with an eight-foot stone wall and a clear view all around."

Roth had been watching Kelly closely, looking for the moron Mundi had described. He could see only focus and intensity. "How'd you find all this out?"

"The site plan is in the Registry of Deeds down in Flemington. Then I got a cabbie to drive me up here and I got out like I was lost and asked for directions."

Roth nodded. No moron so far. "What do you have in mind?"

"Newark's too crowded. This place is tight as a tick, and he's always got his soldiers around him." Kelly accelerated past the drive and turned north on County Road 517. "But you know, I think we could get him anywhere."

"'Get him anywhere' isn't much of a plan."

"King of the Jungle."

"Jungle?"

"He's at the top of the food chain with no natural enemies. He's got these guys protecting him—but they're sleepwalking."

Strange, certainly, but not a moron by any means.

"But you do have a plan."

"I do. Just sit tight." Kelly liked the way Roth had frankly, coldly, sized him up at the diner in Newark, and he appreciated the lack of social bullshit. The guy was built like Primo Carnera, but he obviously had a brain.

They took a right off Route 517 and pulled up in front of the Black Oak Country Club.

"A golf course?"

"Mr. D. and two of his boys play nine on Tuesday and Thursday mornings. Eight thirty tee time. He sends two guys out in the slot in front of him, and two behind."

Kelly drove a few hundred yards down the road, along the rusted chain-link fence with fairway on the other side. When he came to a wooded section, he pulled the car over and got out. Roth followed him up to the fence and under the four-foot flap Kelly had cut in it. They stood in the cool shade of oak and pine trees, surveying the course.

"The first hole is way over there and it goes up to your left. The second one comes back. The third starts down by the entrance, runs up here, and makes a turn—what do they call it?"

"Dogleg. Dogleg right."

"Makes a dogleg right, at these woods here."

Roth got it immediately. "The ground crew, what do they wear?"

"Black T-shirts and khaki pants."

"That shouldn't be too difficult."

"I wouldn't think . . . And a couple of rakes, maybe?"

"And bags."

"Big bags on our shoulders. For the hardware. Right. Rakes and litter bags." Kelly felt like he'd been working with this guy his whole life.

"So tomorrow morning we let the first two go by, pop DiNoto's threesome, and be back in the car before the other two catch up. Is that what you had in mind?"

"Exactly."

Kelly had already procured two stolen pistols with handcrafted silencers the size of beer cans. Roth was given plenty of time to familiarize himself with the gear back in Newark, after they bought their rakes and bags.

Next morning the two of them ambled to within twenty feet of the increasingly surprised threesome, then made their rush. They caught the two goons reaching under their seats in the golf cart for guns. DiNoto never got past "What the fuck?" and he was done. They wiped the guns, put them back in the bags, left the whole mess there, and drove off.

On the turnpike Kelly said, "What he was wearing . . ."

"What who was wearing?"

"Those short little pants."

"Plus fours. They're called plus fours. They used to be part of the costume."

"Oh. Died with his plus fours on."

"Exactly."

Roth was thinking of the old days, when working for Mundi had been fun.

Mailman Hell

The Mailman knew he was in for it, but the precise nature of his suffering surprised him. He'd thought the punishment would consist of physical and psychological distress while he kicked his habit, but the pain was only a means—an instant-by-instant alarm—returning him to the business at hand. His hell consisted of an image of sitting in the room with Langer, his arm beneficently extended, and his smiling nod, "After you, my friend." Over and over and over again it replayed, on the junk-sick plane ride to San Francisco, during the agonizing marches through the Haight, and while he lay awake those endless nights on his cruddy bed at the Y. It was all a dream. Haight-Ashbury was a dream, Golden Gate Park was a dream: the weird chicks, the mist-drenched Pacific light, the hippie hustlers, the down and dirty drag of strange faces, voices, the fear they had of his fear of them. The hookup at the clinic, facilitated by smiling, scary Diggers, was a dream, too. All a dream, all punctuated by nightmare chills and sweats. The only real thing had been handing Langer his death.

He must have known, somehow, that Langer would cook the shit up uncut and poke it into himself. Why had he let it happen?

Was that what Langer'd wanted? Was it assisted suicide? Murder? An innocent mistake? The Mailman's existence took place inside this misery-laden thought loop. Weeks with no relief, accompanied by constant, drumming pain in the throat and neck. He wept from it, welcomed it. Told himself he was getting clean.

Finally he went to the clinic. The doctor, a peach-fuzz kid half his age, wrote down his information, thought for a while, then informed him he wasn't a junkie. He was a recovering cancer patient who'd improperly managed his necessary medication. The diagnosis hit the Mailman like a slap in the face.

The kid put him on a proper med schedule, told him to fill his scrip and come back the next day and take his meds in the clinic.

The Mailman stayed in his room, sweating it out, working his penance.

After two days the kid banged on his door at the Y. "Don't do this to yourself. All you need is a sane environment." He handed the Mailman a list of clinics all over the state.

The Mailman, in underpants and T-shirt, gawked, then closed the door and took the paper with him back to his bed of pain. His throat was killing him. As he scanned the paper and read its list of exotic, Spanish-sounding cities, he realized his throat *would* kill him. For some reason, unknown, he found he didn't want to die just then.

He filled his scrip and showed up at the clinic the next day, waiting forever in a room of sniffling junkies and dead people walking. It felt almost like that day back in Gloucester when he'd tumbled into the new grand scheme. Life had ground his tough, lovely spirit to a nub but not destroyed it. When a tree was chopped down, it sent up saplings. The Langer guilt trip had reached its end. Nothing left there but madness and death.

The Mailman was on his way up for air.

The kid was surprised to see him at the clinic, and his face showed it. The Mailman liked that.

He took out his pad and wrote, "This is not a sane environment."

"You're right. It's not. What do you have in mind?"

The Mailman rasped, "Dangiego."

The kid smiled. "San Diego. That's good. You'll like it there."

As it turned out, the kid was right.

That Was That

Tears welled in Norbert's eyes when Kelly walked into Sammy's. "I knew it. I just fucking knew it." He retreated to the cooler and took a calming breath.

Jarkey stood and stared. He wanted to cry, but something was in the way. He approached his old boss, back from the dead, and launched the sincerest right cross he'd ever attempted in his life, freighted with all the pain and guilt and loss he had in him. Smooth as Ali, feet already perfectly positioned, Kelly jacked his torso out of harm's way. That was that. Then he moved in. They hugged.

Jarkey said, "You fucking asshole."

Kelly said, "I know, I know."

Pepsi had never noticed he was gone, but she was glad to see him now that he was back.

It was sweet for all of them. DiNoto's empire had been torn apart by vicious infighting and was eventually taken over by people who had no beef with Mundi, no grudge about the heroin, no problem with Mr. D. being out of the way. Kelly's friends got their city back.

For Kelly there was still one nagging thing left to do. The package he'd carried out of Gloria Mundi's apartment, the letters he'd studied during his quiet hours in Bensonhurst, demanded an answer.

It took awhile. Phone calls and field trips in the Ford. Jarkey back twice to Genzlinger in the newspaper morgue, so happy to be working again for Kelly that he didn't even voice his obvious question—*Are you out of your fucking mind?*

Finally Kelly had everything lined up the way he wanted it. As far as he was concerned, the timing was perfect. School would be back in session, and Agnes's classmate and Gloria's protector—Dr. Ruth Warfel, dean of women at Bryn Mawr College—would be in her office.

She was tall and angular, wearing a tailored white blouse, gray tweed skirt and matching vest. Kelly sat in an overstuffed armchair on the other side of her desk and looked out the big window behind her onto the rolling lawn, where coeds roamed like browsing does. Kelly realized she was staring at him, expecting him to speak.

He told her that Richard Mundi had hired him because he was worried about the company Gloria was keeping. However, the investigation had taken an unexpected turn. Gloria's apartment had been vandalized by her enemies and certain letters had come into his possession. These letters confirmed past issues he'd suspected. There were unanswered questions about the manner of Agnes Day's death. Serious questions.

She smiled at him, not kindly. "After your initial call I spoke with Gloria. She told me you had performed a valuable, ah, service for her. She urged me to speak with you."

Kelly smiled back, looking for the right in. "That was kind of you both. Thank you."

This produced a surprising effect. The dean's smile fell away and she leaned over the desk at him. "I don't like to be lied to, Mr. Kelly. My call prompted Gloria to look for the letters, and she discovered they'd been stolen. She told me you were the only person with any possible motive for this theft."

Kelly kept silent.

"Think about it, Mr. Kelly. Think how it must have felt to discover that those precious letters, from her dying mother, were gone. Think of the sense of violation."

"You've got it all wrong, Dean Warfel."

"Do I? Who else on the planet would have any interest in Gloria's relationship with her mother? Certainly not the Mafia."

"Listen, I saw the inscriptions in those yearbooks, and I've read the letters. I know how close you and Agnes were, and how close you are with Gloria, too."

"What of it?"

"Mundi double-crossed me. Tried to have me killed. I believe it was because of what I learned about Agnes's death."

Her expression tightened. "These are tragic, entirely private family matters, Mr. Kelly."

Kelly hesitated, then decided it was time his cards were on the table. "I'm just a guy who stumbled across some unpleasant truths. I think you can tell me what Agnes was talking about when she told you death was pursuing her. It's all over the letters."

"Agnes had a habit of poetic expression, Mr. Kelly, and she was unflinchingly aware of the fate that stalked her. I will not have you speak in this manner." She stared at him curiously. "What don't you understand?"

"Come off it, Dean. It was Mundi, wasn't it? He had her killed or drove her to her death somehow. What was going on in that family? I've taken this all the way to the end, but it won't go any farther. I just need to know. Who killed her and why?"

Ruth Warfel continued to stare at him, hard, as if she were scrutinizing a strange life-form. He could see the hostility drain from her, replaced by something more neutral. But also more dismissive. "Mr. Kelly, I never wanted this meeting. When I spoke with Gloria, she told me how you became involved with her father, what happened to you, and how you subsequently, ah, corrected the situation. She told me honestly what she thought of you and urged me to speak with you. To request that you return those letters. That's the reason, the only reason, for this meeting. You have consistently, completely, and willfully misconstrued every bit of intelligence regarding her mother that has come your way. You've now lied to me, and it's clear that if you truly believe your overimaginative hypothesis, you must be lying to yourself, because the facts do not support it."

Kelly started to reply, but she cut him off. "Agnes Day Mundi died of congenital heart failure, Mr. Kelly. She led a brave, uncompromising life, and she was deeply mourned by her husband, her daughter, and by me. I want you to return those letters immediately. And then I expect to have heard the last of you. Now get out of this office."

She seemed to mean business. Kelly picked up his hat and departed.

By the time he got back to his office, the true import of his interview was beginning to sink in. Since his return from the dead he'd been sorting through his ransacked belongings, slowly putting everything back in order. He resumed this activity, in a meditative way, as he pictured Ruth Warfel and what a surprisingly tough customer she'd turned out to be.

He decided that she'd probably been telling the truth about Agnes Day Mundi. He could see, now, that he might've misinterpreted a few things about Agnes's past and her relationship with Mundi. All the stuff about death stalking was hard to interpret. But he had to admit that if she'd thought her husband had been trying to kill her, she'd have written something to her old friend along the lines of, "My husband is trying to kill me." Well, it wasn't the first time he'd ever been wrong.

He found Mundi's case file in the ungainly stack waiting to be restored to the metal cabinets. There, amid Jarkey's photographs, was a white envelope. It had a familiar look, and he opened it expectantly. Inside were eight $100 bills. He remembered Mundi handing it to him, but he was sure it had contained $1,000. Now *there* was a puzzler. Kelly flipped through the 8 x 10 glossies of Gloria and Gallagher, mulling it over. Then he had an image of Harry Jarkey reaching up to receive two C-notes all those months ago, making some crack about hearing the money talking. He smiled contentedly. Another mystery solved.

Then the phone rang.

It was Julius Roth.

He had an interesting proposition.

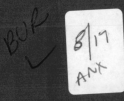